PRO SE PRESS

THE PRANKSTER OF OZ
A Pro Se Productions Publication

All rights reserved under U.S. and International copyright law. This book is licensed only for the private use of the purchaser. May not be copied, scanned, digitally reproduced, or printed for re-sale, may not be uploaded on shareware or free sites, or used in any other manner without the express written permission of the author and/or publisher. Thank you for respecting the hard work of the author.

Written by John R Rose
Editing by Aubrey Stephens and Braden Steel and Maddy Drake

Cover by Larry Nadolsky
Book Design by Antonino Lo Iacono
New Pulp Logo Design by Sean E. Ali
New Pulp Seal Design by Cari Reese

Pro Se Productions, LLC
133 1/2 Broad Street
Batesville, AR, 72501
870-834-4022

editorinchief@prose-press.com
www.prose-press.com

THE PRANKSTER OF OZ
Copyright © 2017 John R Rose

DEDICATION

This story is dedicated to my wife,
Meredith A. Rose.
Thanks!

CONTENTS

1	Chapter One The Mule at The Auction	1
2	Chapter Two The Flying Windmil	15
3	Chapter Three Ozma's Magic Picture	25
4	Chapter Four The Baling Wire Dog	31
5	Chapter Five The Woot Wagon	45
6	Chapter Six Riders of the Blue Sage	55
7	Chapter Seven The Marsh Monster	69
8	Chapter Eight The Prankster at Last!	81
9	Chapter Nine The Racing Hogs!	91
10	Chapter Ten The Magic Cowgirl	107

11	Chapter Eleven The Burley Bear	115
12	Chapter Twelve Turmoil in the Caverns	121
13	Chapter Thirteen The Guardian of the Waterfall	133
14	Chapter Fourteen Traveling the Illumator Transporter	145
15	Chapter Fifteen The Magic Book is Missing!	155
16	Chapter Sixteen Callie and the Magic Book	163
17	Chapter Seventeen The Golden Box	175
18	Chapter Eighteen Pieces of the Puzzle	183
19	Chapter Nineteen The Emerald City	189
20	Chapter Twenty All's Well That Ends Well	197
	About The Author	204

CHAPTER ONE:
THE MULE AT THE AUCTION

The windswept prairie town of Wellsford lay silent and dark under an early morning sky. Another hot Kansas summer day was about to blossom.

Barnaby Amos Fields awoke in the predawn darkness to the aroma of frying bacon, coffee, and scrambled eggs wafting up the stairs to the second floor bedroom. A soft breeze moaned slightly in the backyard evergreens, giving notice to a windy day in the making.

The retired wheat farmer swung his feet to the floor and began pulling on his overalls. Barney muttered under his breath as he headed for the stairs leading to the kitchen and his first cup of Bertha's hot coffee.

"Blasted wind," he grumbled as he tentatively sampled the hot brew. "Always blowing. Never stops. Didn't use to be this way."

"Now, Barney," his wife said, shooting him a reproachful look. "It's no different now than before you retired. You just notice it more."

Barney grunted and sipped his coffee as Bertha placed his breakfast before him. "Know what?" he said, as he began eating. "If it weren't for Frank running the farm now, I'd come out of retirement so fast it'd make your head swim! But I just can't take it back from the boy."

"No, you can't," Bertha agreed firmly. "To begin with, you're too old to do all that work anymore. And, secondly, our son deserves his chance with the farm now. Even more importantly, we want our grandchildren growing up on a farm, not in some big city like Wichita or Topeka."

"Well, I dunno..." Barney began.

"Now, Barney, we discussed this months ago. The decision was made and agreed on then. You just need to get used to taking it easy."

Barney snorted in good-natured disagreement. Then he added, "What I need is a little excitement. Yep," he mused, "just a smidgen."

"Barney," said Bertha, wiping her hands on the tea towel draped over her shoulder. "I've got an idea. They're holding the Miller auction today. It's down at the old bus garage. Why don't you go? Bet you'd get a real kick out of it!"

"Oh, I dunno," Barney protested mildly. "I don't much hold with farm auctions. Seems like taking advantage of somebody else's misfortune."

"Oh, Barney, you know better than that! You just don't know how to relax and enjoy yourself. Go mingle with the crowd. You'll know blame near everybody there."

"Well, I might wander down," Barney conceded.

"Good," replied Bertha. "Now, get yourself out of my way for a while." She turned back to the kitchen sink. "Oh, the auction starts about ten o'clock," she added.

Barney reached for the coffee pot and refilled his cup. He rose from his chair and stretched. "That was a mighty good breakfast, Bertha," he said.

Picking up his cup, he opened the screen door and stepped onto the darkened front porch. It was getting lighter in the east as Barney sat down on the top porch step, holding the hot cup in both hands. Maybe this retirement wasn't so bad after all.

Clarence, the tomcat, rubbed against the leg of his overalls and began to purr.

***

Barney mingled with the crowd around the bus garage and the city park. All kinds of items were laid out on the tables for potential buyers to look at before the auction actually started. The retired farmer checked over the machinery and decided he'd best not look too long or he'd start thinking about buying.

Pulling out his pocketknife and picking up a small stick from the ground, Barney began to whittle as he walked. Then he stopped at a table and looked at a box of little books. They were chubby little books and had originally sold for a dime in the five and ten stores. Barney grinned as he flipped through the pages. The books were half pictures and half print.

"Must be two or three dozen," he murmured to himself.

"Huh? What'd you say, Barney?" came a voice.

"Oh, morning, Matthew," replied Barney, putting down the little book he was holding in the hand with the pocketknife. "Just talking to myself. Didn't know anybody was listening."

"Wasn't trying to eavesdrop," Matthew replied good-naturedly.

"Well, how are things going?" Barney asked. "Been a while since I've seen you."

"Oh, could be a lot better, you know. Been kind of rough since Rachel passed on, bless her soul." Matthew hesitated, and then continued. "That cancer was real tough on her. The pain. And it took every penny we had. The bills, you know. The hospital and the funeral." Matthew looked at Barney and forced a smile. "I'll get along. Always have."

Shouting at the far end of the block interrupted the conversation of the two old friends. The town deputy had two men in his grip and was ushering them toward the railroad tracks at the north edge of town.

"Looks like those two bums I saw earlier this morning," Matthew commented.

"Well, I reckon Joe's got things well in hand," Barney laughed.

"I dunno," Matthew replied. "They had a young boy with them this morning. Don't see him anywhere."

"A young one? Hoboes don't usually have kids with them."

"These two did. Boy about twelve, I'd say. Looked just as scruffy as either one of those two fellows."

The auctioneer started his spiel on what a great day it was and what great items were up for bid. Barney and Matthew drifted apart.

It was close to noon when the auctioneer reached the box of little books and began to praise their condition and value.

"...lots of westerns and jungle and cartoon books here," he rattled away in his singsong voice. "Must be forty books in this box," he continued. "What am I bid for the whole box? Make some young fellow a fine little library. Anybody start with a five dollar bill?"

Light laughter rippled through the crowd as the auctioneer launched into his rapid-fire delivery. But there were no bids. Five dollars was more than the books had cost when they were new.

"All right, my friends," the auctioneer called. "Who'll give me two-fifty to get the bidding started?" Silence followed his plea.

"Say, Barney," he called over the crowd to the old farmer, who sat whittling in the shade of a tree. "I saw you looking at these books earlier. You know what fine shape they are in, almost like new. Now, how about bidding a dollar just to get things going?"

Barney nodded and the auctioneer again started his rapid-fire delivery. However, there were no more bids and the farmer soon became the owner of the box of Big Little Books.

A short time later Barney closed his pocketknife and slipped it back into the pocket of his overalls. Then he reached into the bib pocket, took out a dollar bill, and sauntered over to the clerk. He handed her the money and picked up the box of books.

"Mighty heavy reading there, Barney," the clerk joked, as she checked the item on her list as having been paid.

"Yep," Barney replied. "Figure I'll give these to Fred, Jr."

"Oh," replied the clerk, "is Fred in school yet?"

"No, not yet," Barney answered. "Will be next fall, though. I figure he can get in a lot of good coloring until he's old enough to read 'em."

"Bet he has a lot of fun," the clerk replied.

Barney walked over to the tent area where food was being sold. He purchased a sandwich and a coke before returning to his bench in the shade of the tree.

The perpetual wind of the last few days had died down. Storm clouds loomed threateningly in the west. The stillness was almost eerie, when the auctioneer was silent.

Barney set his box of books down and placed the sandwich on top of them. He took a drink of his soda pop and leaned back against the tree trunk. Bertha was right, he thought, this was turning out to be an enjoyable day. Then, from the corner of his eye, he caught a glimpse of a moving shadow.

Barney's left hand flicked out and caught the wrist of a young boy who was reaching for his sandwich. For a few seconds the two just looked at each other. Then the boy tried to pull away, but Barney just tightened his grip.

"Sit down, son," the old farmer said. "You look a mite hungry. Care to share my sandwich?"

Barney tugged on the boy's wrist, and the lad quickly sat down by the box of books. Carefully the farmer unwrapped the sandwich and handed the boy half of it.

The youngster ate ravenously. His clothes were ragged and his head of tousled hair was unkempt.

Be a nice looking boy, Barney thought, *if he were cleaned up a bit.*

When the lad had eaten the first half of the sandwich, Barney quietly handed him the second half. The boy took the offering and quickly ate it.

"What's your name, son?" Barney asked.

"Name's Billy," the youngster replied, wiping a grimy hand across his mouth.

"Billy," Barney said. "Now that's a nice name. Have you got a last name?"

"I don't think so," Billy replied, his brows knitted in deep thought. "No," he said, his face brightening, "I don't have one."

"All right," replied Barney, deciding not to push the issue. "So, what brings you to town? The auction?"

"No," said Billy. "Just passing through." Then, with wistfulness in his voice, he added, "With a couple of friends."

"Oh, I see," Barney nodded. "Are your friends around here?"

"Yeah, they're here somewhere," Billy

answered, beginning to look the crowd over in search of his comrades.

After a moment of silence, Barney spoke again. "These friends, were they a pair of bums?"

Billy drew a sharp breath. "They, sir, are gentlemen of the open road!"

"Well, that may be," Barney agreed. "However, I did see two men being escorted to the edge of town a while ago. I believe they hopped the freight train that came through about eleven o'clock."

Billy's face went white. He swallowed hard. Looking at the ground, the young boy kicked at a tuft of grass.

"Guess I'm on my own," he finally said in a hoarse whisper.

"Would seem so," the farmer agreed.

"They been telling me for some time now that they was gonna leave me behind. Claimed that someday they'd get in trouble because of me bein' so young!" Billy's voice broke and he gave a stifled sob. "I just never believed they'd really do it."

Barney reached out to pat the lad on the back in sympathy.

"You no good cheats!" came a high pitched voice from near the clerk's table. "I didn't buy no blasted mule!"

Barney and Billy, along with the rest of the crowd, turned to see what had brought on the commotion. There by the table, his face beet red and one arm waving in the air, stood old Matthew Mosley. Next to him stood a man holding the tether of a mule.

"Come on," said Barney, picking up his box of

books. "Let's go see what this is all about."

As they neared the table, old Matthew, his hands shoved deep in his overall pockets, kicked an empty chair.

"You're all a bunch of crooks!" he shouted. There were tears streaming down the old man's face. "Just a bunch of blasted thieves!"

"Matt!" shouted Barney, as he neared the scene. "What's the matter?"

"Aw, Barney, these nuts are trying to say I bid on and bought this broken down old mule!" Matthew Mosley pulled out a big red bandana and wiped his perspiring face.

Barney looked at the auction workers. The clerk was on her feet and the man holding the mule was trying not to lose his temper.

"It's recorded right here," the clerk said in a voice that was somewhat shaky. "Now, there may have been a mistake somewhere..."

"Mistake!" yelled Matthew. "Ain't no mistake! You guys are just a bunch of rips!"

The worker holding the mule doubled up his fist and clenched his teeth in anger.

"How much was the winning bid?" Barney asked.

"Five bucks!" Matthew exploded. "Five bucks I don't have! And if I did, I sure the dickens wouldn't spend it on some slab-sided old mule!"

Barney reached into the bib pocket of his overalls and pulled out his billfold. He counted out five one dollar bills and handed them to the clerk.

Matthew sat down on the chair he had recently kicked and held his head in his hands.

"Thanks, Barney," he said. "You're a true friend. I'll pay you back sometime. Whenever I get on my feet again."

"Forget it, Matthew," Barney replied. "That's what friends are for."

Barney led the mule away from the crowd. Billy followed, carrying the box of books. For the next hour they stayed in the shade of a tree not far from the clerk's table hoping the real bidder would show up for the animal. But no one came.

"Well, Billy," Barney finally said, "those storm clouds are getting bigger and darker by the minute. Going to be raining in less time than it takes to tell about it. Better get this mule to my barn before we all get soaked."

There was a bit of lightning in the west and thunder rumbled as if to punctuate the man's statement.

Barney looked at the young boy with his hand on the halter of the old mule. "I think I'd better take my purchases and head for home. Want to come along?"

"Yeah, might as well," the lad replied. "Got no other place to go."

The old farmer led the mule and young Billy carried the box of Big Little Books.

"These little books sure look interesting," the boy commented as they walked along. "Especially this one with the happy dragon on the cover."

Barney glanced toward the boy. He was holding a small book in one hand while the other arm was wrapped around the box.

"Oh, yeah. *The Laughing Dragon of Oz*," the

farmer said, looking at the title. "Want to read it?"

"Uh, yeah...or, uh, well, I guess not," the boy mumbled. "Don't really have time."

Barney knew at that moment the boy couldn't read.

"Did you say, '*Oz*'?" came a deep, smooth voice.

The farmer felt the hair on the back of his neck stand up. The boy's eyes grew large and round. The man and the boy looked about but no one was near them. The gravel covered street was empty. Barney felt his knees go weak and he reached out to steady himself by placing a hand on the neck of the mule.

"You *did* say, '*Oz*,' didn't you?" The mule turned his head to look at Barney, and the farmer took a quick step backwards as he realized the voice was that of the mule.

"You talked," he stammered.

"Indeed," the beast replied. "Now, let us move on toward that barn you mentioned earlier. There is one gully washer of a storm brewing."

With that, the wind, which had died down earlier, began to pick up again. A large raindrop bounced off the mule's nose, as if to emphasize the fact.

The mule began to walk and Barney clung to the animal's neck to keep from collapsing on the spot. Billy began to follow along as though he were in a trance, his movements very mechanical.

"Now, then," the mule began talking again and Barney tightened his grip. The farmer's whole body seemed to be turning to jelly. "You fellows have a book about Oz, right?"

Billy and Barney both nodded. The mule brayed like a normal mule and Barney immediately felt better.

"Sorry," apologized the mule. "When I try to laugh, I just get that gosh-awful mule sound. It's part of the hex." He turned his head to look at Barney and then turned the other way to look at Billy.

"Okay, fellows," said the mule. "You were talking about an Oz book."

"Uh-huh," said Barney. "It was *The Laughing Dragon of Oz*." He reached across the mule's neck and Billy handed the little book to him.

"Oh, I don't need to see it," the mule said. "What I need is someone who believes in Oz. Do you believe in the magical land of Oz?"

"After all that has happened today," Barney sighed, "I could believe in anything."

"Yeah, me, too," chimed in Billy.

"I remember Bertha reading Oz books to our kids when they were little," Barney said as he absentmindedly tucked the little book into the bib pocket of his overalls.

"If you fellows believe," said the mule, "that is, truly believe, the first step is done."

"What do you mean?" asked Barney.

They had arrived at the sidewalk leading to the porch of Barney's house. The windows were open but the door was closed and the lights were off, so Barney knew Bertha was still attending her afternoon meeting.

"Here," said the old farmer, changing the subject, "I'll put those books up on the porch where they won't get wet. You take the mule down to the barn, Billy. I'll be down directly."

Clarence, the tom cat, left the shade of the lilac bush and trotted along beside Barnaby Fields as he carried the box of books to the shelter of the porch. He had completely forgotten the little book in his bib pocket.

CHAPTER TWO:
THE FLYING WINDMILL

The strong wind made Barney clutch tightly at his hat as he leaned into the gusting force of nature and hurried toward the barn. The droplets of rain, driven by the force of the wind, stung when they hit Barney's unprotected cheek.

"Boy, this is going to be a bad one," he muttered. Then remembering the open windows, he turned and hurried back to the house. It didn't take long for him to close the windows, upstairs and down, then he remembered the little books on the porch. The rain was coming down in sheets now.

Barney stepped onto the porch, picked up the book box, and returned with it to the kitchen table. Looking out the window, he could see nothing through the gray downpour. Lightning crackled in the sky followed immediately by the deafening boom of thunder.

"That was close," he exclaimed out loud.

He opened the door and stepped outside onto the porch. Looking toward the barn, he could barely make out the dark outline of the huge building.

Then, glancing up the road, he saw a dark object moving toward him. Whoever that is ought to have his lights on, he thought. Then Barney's jaw dropped in surprise.

"That's the neighbor's horse tank rolling along there!" he exclaimed. "Hey, it's headed right toward the barn!"

Without a second thought, Barney jerked his hat down tightly and raced into the downpour toward the rolling metal tank. Angling across the yard and hopping over the yard fence, the old man raced to intercept the round rolling water tank. His efforts were to no avail.

Watching from the barn door were Billy and the recently acquired talking mule.

"We'd better help Barney!" shouted Billy running into the rain to join the farmer. The mule hesitated only briefly before he, too, raced to join in the effort to stop the tank.

Pushing and shoving at the rapidly rolling tank, the trio managed to change its direction enough that it missed the barn by a matter of inches.

"Good work!" shouted Barney through the rain as the tank continued to roll. "Hard tellin' where that thing's gonna stop!" he called to his water soaked companions. "I... hey! That tank is going to hit the windmill!" The farmer broke into a sprint trying to catch the horse tank again. Behind him came the boy and the mule.

They caught up with the tank just as it reached the windmill and careened off one of the legs. The force of the collision broke the wooden leg of the old mill and the rolling tank tipped over and landed on its bottom a few feet away. Barney and Billy went tumbling.

"Hold that tank down!" Barney shouted, leaping to his feet with agility that belied his age.

Together the farmer and the boy grasped the rim of the tank and used their weight in an attempt to keep it on the ground. The mule came over, gently reared up and hopped into the tank.

"That's the idea!" exclaimed the farmer. He clamored into the tank followed by his young friend.

"Guess we're already wet," Barney chuckled. "Might as well keep this thing anchored 'til the wind dies down."

"Reckon so," Billy replied.

The mule folded his knees and lay down in the center of the tank. Billy, his shaggy head of hair wet and matted, sat down and leaned back against the mule, his face tilted to the pelting rain, eyes closed.

There was a bright flash of lightning followed by the earsplitting rumble of thunder. Then, through the howling wind, came the scraping tearing sound of metal against metal. The occupants of the tank had instinctively ducked when the bolt struck, but now Billy looked up. Through the rain and in the flickering glow of the lightning, Barney saw the boy's face blanch white.

Looking quickly to the sky, the farmer saw the

top metal section of the windmill toppling toward them.

"Duck!" he yelled, diving toward the boy and mule, covering his head with his arms as he did so.

Lightning crackled across the sky again, almost blinding in its brightness. The tumbling windmill section turned an iridescent bluish color as it was enveloped by the electrical power of the storm. Then, without cause or reason, the falling windmill section flipped again and landed directly in the horse tank. The iridescent light surrounding the wheel and vane spread down the mills legs and engulfed the water tank.

Barney's eyes were wide with disbelief as the glow covered him. At first there was a tingling sensation and the hair on his neck stood up. This was followed by a wave of heat and then a strange feeling of ice cold wires running through his body.

"My blood must be freezing," he muttered as his head tilted forward and his chin came to rest on his chest. Barney lost consciousness as the pounding rain continued.

When the farmer regained his senses, he was lying flat on his back looking up at the twinkling stars.

"Oh, mi'gosh," he muttered, his hands reaching to cradle his throbbing head. "What a horrible nightmare!"

Barney gave an instantaneous reflexive jerk as he realized he was looking upward through a section of the windmill watching the wind vane and the mill wheel whirling around and around.

Then he relaxed. It was *not* falling. It was just

simply running. Probably pumping water to Bertha's garden.

The old farmer grunted and rolled over thinking he would get up and go into the house for a cup of coffee. His hand clutched a hairy leg and he gave another involuntary start.

"Got to get myself under control," he said, shaking his head. "That nightmare has me jumpier than a hop toad."

"Me, too," came a small, frightened voice.

Barney held his breath and slowly looked over his shoulder as the realization that he had not been dreaming came over him.

"That you, Billy?" he asked.

"Yeah," replied the trembling voice.

"Well," continued the farmer, "we've been in this tank too long. Let's get out and go up to the house and get warmed up. It's already dark and the rain has let up."

"Mr. Barney," came the boy's soft voice, using the old farmer's name for the first time, "we can't get out."

"The boy is right," came a deep voice. Barney again felt a weird sensation travel through his body as he realized the mule had spoken.

"Why not?" he asked, climbing stiffly to his feet. The wild race in the rain chasing the horse tank wasn't something his body was in the habit of doing.

"We're floating in the sky," the lad replied numbly. "Ground must be about a mile below us."

Barney stepped over to the side of the horse tank, then grasped the edge with both hands as he looked into a deep void of darkness. Above him the windmill ran with a steady whirring sound and Barney could tell from the wind in his face that they were sailing or flying along at a very rapid rate of speed.

His knees seemed to turn to jelly and Barney slowly folded into a sitting position, his back against the side of the tank.

In the dull gray light of the coming dawn, the old farmer could see the staves of the windmill legs from the top section. They seemed to be fastened solidly to the tank. Then Barney remembered the lightning and the blue glow and the contrasting sensations that went with the experience.

"Windmill seems to be welded to the tank," he said, not particularly directing his thoughts to either the boy or the mule. Neither answered.

Eventually the occupants of the flying horse tank drifted into a deep unnatural sleep.

Barney awoke with bright sunlight streaming in his face. He blinked and looked about him. He decided it must be about an hour after sunrise. The boy and the mule were both sound asleep. Quietly Barney got to his feet and stepped to the edge of the gently rocking tank, expecting to see the ground far below. Instead he found himself looking at beautiful blue water that gently lapped against the edges as it rocked the horse tank. Not far away was a grassy green bank and just beyond were the tall trees of a forest. The tank was slowly being washed toward the shore. Looking in all directions, the old farmer decided they must be on a lake.

Choosing not to awaken his companions until

they could go ashore, Barney stood at the edge of the tank gazing toward the trees just up the slope from the lake. As they approached land, he began to make out a path or narrow road leading up the hill and into the stand of trees.

"Roads always go somewhere," he said reflectively to himself.

A few moments later, the tank gently nudged against the sand bar at the shore line of the lake. Barney turned and softly shook Billy's shoulder and then rubbed the mule on the forehead. Both awoke immediately.

"We have arrived," said Barney, with a shake of his head. "I have no idea where, but we are here!"

Billy climbed over the edge of the tank immediately and the mule, with one hop, was right behind him. Neither wished to stay in the tank any longer than necessary.

"Oh, my aching bones," complained Barney as he, too, climbed over the edge of the tank.

"What now?" asked Billy.

"Well, you see that road?" replied Barney. "It has to go somewhere. Let's find out where and how long it's going to take us to get back to Kansas."

"You, my friend," said Billy, with a big smile on his face, "are feeling the call of the open road! Yes, sir!"

The three companions walked quickly up the road to the edge of the forest which was much taller and darker than it had appeared from the shoreline. Barney stopped and looked back.

"Hey, look!" he said in surprise. The boy and mule turned to see the windmill-horse tank floating away across the lake. "I should have thought to tie it down," said the farmer.

"With what?" came the mule's deep voice. "And, perhaps more importantly, why? Were you planning to get back in that thing?"

With a chuckle, Barney and his friends turned and followed the winding path into the forest.

They had not gone far, when young Billy, who was hopping and skipping along, suddenly fell flat on his face. He rolled over, sat up and began tugging at something around his ankle.

"Here, let me help you," exclaimed Barney bending over the boy's foot. "Well, it's nothing more than a tangled bit of baling wire. Must have fallen off a truck as I sure don't see any fences hereabouts."

"Throw the stuff away!" exclaimed Billy. "It's just a nuisance."

"Oh, no," replied Barney, "baling wire is very important to a farmer. You just don't throw it away! It can always be used for something." The farmer took the wire and began straightening out the tangled mess as they walked along.

"You know," said Billy, "is it my imagination or does everything around here have a blue tint to it?"

They had not gone far enough into the forest but what Barnaby Fields could look back and see the blue lake and the blue sky. The grass over which they had walked did seem to have a blueness to it, but it was not much different than western Kansas bluestem. He looked at the trees with their dark leaves and even darker trunks and limbs. There did seem to be a definite shading of blue color. It was not extremely noticeable but was definitely there.

"You're right, Billy," said the farmer. "What kind of strange place have we stumbled into?"

CHAPTER THREE: OZMA'S MAGIC PICTURE

The Emerald City is the capital of the Land of Oz. It is located in the middle of the fairyland and is primarily constructed of green marble. Vast numbers of emeralds of varying shapes and sizes have been magically placed in these great slabs of marble, giving the city its radiant green glow.

The Emerald City itself has approximately ten thousand buildings which house a population in excess of fifty-seven thousand inhabitants. While the outside of the buildings and streets contain only emeralds, the interiors of the structures are decorated with many different kinds of precious and beautiful stones. Rubies, turquoises, amethysts, diamonds and sapphires abound, glittering and twinkling as they cast a soft radiance throughout the thousands of homes and businesses within the

Emerald City.

Located in the exact center of this wonderful city was the Royal Palace of Princess Ozma, the girl ruler of Oz. The palace contained a number of large towers and had numerous small minarets, spires and turrets giving it a very grand appearance. From a distance, the castle could be seen sparkling in the light of the setting sun.

Inside the palace Princess Ozma sat on her magnificently designed throne, deeply absorbed by her thoughts. The last of the kingdom's matters had been taken care of for the day. The orchestra from the dome had taken its leave for the remainder of the evening and the two great beasts, the Cowardly Lion and the Hungry Tiger that presided on either side of the young ruler during Throne Room sessions had gone to their stables for the evening feed. She smiled to herself.

A shadow in the doorway caused Ozma to look up. Across the marbled floor of the Throne Room stood Jellia Jamb, the palace housekeeper, with a parchment in her hand. She waved gaily to the young princess.

"A message from Glinda the Good," she called across the room. "Are you leaving or do you want me to bring it to you?"

Ozma stood and smiled at her jubilant maid. "I'll come get it, Jellia," she replied.

The girl gave a curtsy and placed the parchment in the outstretched hand of her ruler. "The message was delivered to Captain General Omby Amby, who brought it to me and I to you," smiled the maid. "Now if you would excuse me, I have some cleaning I must attend to." Ozma nodded and Jellia Jamb was on her way. Keeping the great palace spotlessly clean was the maid's one goal in life.

For a long while, the ruler of Oz looked at the parchment. It was, indeed, a message from Glinda, the Good Witch of the South, ruler of the Quadlings, and close friend of Ozma.

The youthful princess returned to her throne where she studied the message. It seemed to be a normal letter in all respects. It had been delivered in a 'non-rush' manner and the note itself bore no resemblance to urgency. Yet something seemed to compel Ozma to look again. Was there something she was supposed to be reading between the lines? Why did she get a feeling of such urgency?

Glinda was asking that she come to her castle and go through some of the items in the Great Book of Records. This huge book of magic, as you know, keeps track of every single thing that takes place in Oz and records it within the pages. One simply has to be able to find that particular bit of recorded history to know what has taken place. And it is recorded there within seconds of the time it actually occurs.

Princess Ozma arose from her throne. Her mind was made up. She would go to Glinda the Good at once. She gave a pull on a silken cord and a silvery note sounded through the halls of Royal Palace. A servant appeared from the shadows.

Ozma gave instructions for the Sawhorse to be hitched to the red coach immediately and to meet her at the palace steps. Then she turned to her own private quarters where she went directly to a set of rich velvet curtains hanging on one wall. Taking hold of the golden cord she pulled them open revealing a large picture hanging on the wall displaying a pleasant pastoral scene. This was the Magic Picture residing in an emerald frame that could show the activities of any person at any time when asked.

"Show me Woot the Wanderer," the young ruler asked. Immediately the peaceful scene on the wall swirled as though being tossed about by the wind. Then it settled down and the image of a teenage boy came into focus. The youngster was sitting by a small fire in the forest and seemed to roasting hickory nuts. All appeared well with him.

Ozma used the Magic Picture to check the whereabouts and wellbeing of several other citizens of Oz. Then she asked for her final request.

"Show me Captain Fyter," said the princess and the picture on the wall changed again bringing into view a tin soldier. As the image cleared, it became obvious that the fellow was in some type of predicament, as he seemed to be bound hand and foot. Since the darkness of night had settled over Oz, it was somewhat difficult to make out the surroundings of both Woot the Wanderer and of Captain Fyter.

"I wonder," said the little princess, "if Captain Fyter is really in any danger that he cannot get himself out of or not. Perhaps I should send word to his old friend, Nick Chopper, and let him decide if something should be done."

She pulled the cord on the velvet drapes to cover the Magic Picture. "Yes," she said as she turned to leave the room, "that is what I shall do."

The Emerald Castle was breathtakingly beautiful in the shadowy corridors with the hundreds of thousands of gems gleaming in the subdued light. Princess Ozma, not quite sure why she was in such a rush, hurried toward the front steps of the palace and the waiting Sawhorse with the red coach.

As yet she had not dispatched anyone with a message for the Tin Woodman, also known as Nick Chopper, concerning his old friend Captain Fyter. The Sawhorse was just coming around the corner from the stables with the red coach when Ozma appeared on the top steps. She stopped for a moment. There was no one else in sight and she did not want to leave the task of sending a messenger to the tin man to the servants in the castle.

"I'll have Omby Amby take care of the matter when we go through the gates," she said as she started down the steps. "Where is a messenger when you need one?"

"Right here," came two different voices, one on her left and the other on her right. The Shaggy Man was on her left where no one had been a moment before and on the right of the princess was the Hungry Tiger.

Ozma laughed lightly. "Either of you may take my message to the Tin Woodman at his castle in the Winkie Country. Just tell him the Magic Picture shows Captain Fyter, who is up in the Gillikin Country, to be in some sort of trouble. I would like for Nick to check on his old buddy if he has the time." She explained for a moment the situation as she had observed it in the Magic Picture.

Princess Ozma waved quickly to the Shaggy Man and the Hungry Tiger and climbed into the red coach. A short command to the Sawhorse and she was rapidly disappearing from the scene.

"Well," said the Shaggy Man, "do we draw straws to see who goes?"

"Why don't we both go?" suggested the tiger. "I am much stronger and faster than you, but you can ride on my back when you get tired."

"That sounds like a plan to me," replied the Shaggy Man. "How long before you will be ready to go?"

"I'm ready now," was the reply. "And you, my friend?"

"Likewise," answered the Shaggy Man. "I just want to pick up some apples as we pass by the orchards outside the emerald gates."

With that, the two friends began a rapid walk toward the east entrance to the Emerald City. The castle of the Tin Woodman was several days distance and they were eager to be on their way.

CHAPTER FOUR:
THE BALING WIRE DOG

"I'm hungry," said Billy as they walked along the trail in the dark forest. "Do you think we'll come to a house or a town or something pretty soon?"

"I sure don't know," replied Barney, "but I could really use a cup of coffee and some of Bertha's pancakes about now!"

"Yeah, me too!" exclaimed the lad, although he had never met Bertha, nor had he ever eaten any of her pancakes.

The farmer, with the roll of baling wire hung over his shoulder, looked toward the sky and the overhead sun. The tall dark trees blocked most of the glaring sunlight, but Barney was just checking to see what time it was.

"It's about twelve-thirty. Let's stop and rest for a little bit," Barney said, pointing toward a log lying beside the trail not far in front of them. "If someone doesn't come by or if we don't reach a town or something in the next half hour, I'd say we'd better start trying to find food here in the forest somewhere."

The man and boy sat down on the log to rest. The mule stopped and began cropping grass that grew along the side of the road they were following. It felt good to sit down and Barney was aware that he wasn't used to walking so much at one time.

"Say," said the farmer, addressing the mule just a few steps away, "you never did tell us your name, my friend."

The mule looked up, still chewing a mouthful of grass. He moved toward the log, swallowed the grass, and, with a grunt, folded his knees and lay down on the ground in front of the man and boy.

"My name," he said in his deep soft voice, "is Two-Bits and this is my story. What you see in front of you is a mule. Actually, I'm a reindeer, a retired reindeer from the various teams that pull the magic sleigh for Santa Claus. I came to Oz to visit a friend of mine and I ran afoul of a man known as the Prankster."

Barney and Billy had such incredulous looks on their faces that Two-Bits brayed out loud. Then he blinked his eyes and wriggled his ears.

"I am sorry my friends, but as you know," the mule explained, "I can talk. However, my laugh comes out in a gosh-awful mule sound!" He shook his head and rolled his eyes.

"But on with the story," he said. "The Prankster thought it would be funny to turn me into a mule.

He did. I was so disgusted that my first act was to plant my rear hooves against the seat of his pants! He didn't think that was funny! Not one little bit! The next thing I knew, I was encased in blue fire and the Prankster was in the process of sending me to earth. His last words were that I should find someone who believed in Oz before I could return. I was in your world for what seemed to be a very long time!"

Barney and Billy sat silently, not knowing what to say, or even what to believe. Finally the farmer spoke.

"Two-Bits," he began, "you spoke as though we are no longer in our world! Just where are we?"

"Well, I think we are back in Oz," replied Two-Bits. "You see, your world and the magic Land of Oz do not exist in the same dimension anymore. You can't just wander back and forth like in the old times. It's really difficult to go from one world to the other now. I think the Prankster was doing it by going through the Kingdom of Kris Kringle, otherwise known as Santa Claus. You understand, of course, that Santa Claus's North Pole is on a different plane of existence, too."

Barney and Billy were still very confused. Two-Bits looked at them and brayed softly.

"I think our flying horse tank," the mule continued, "probably crossed Kringle's Kingdom in the flight last night. I'm fairly certain we're back in Oz, but I'm not very sure just where. The main objective now is to locate the Prankster and force him to remove the magic spell he has put on me!"

"Do you think we are in Oz?" Billy asked,

looking at Barney.

"I don't know," replied the farmer. "I reckon we'll just have to take the word of Two-Bits on that matter. I'm more than a little confused!"

"You two are somewhat tired," commented the mule. "In my present form, I haven't even drawn a deep breath yet, so to speak. How about hopping on my back and let's continue down this road. The sooner we get moving, the sooner we are likely to find food for you fellows!" The mule stood up.

Barney and Billy looked at each other and then climbed onto the mule's back. In another moment they were moving down the road at a much more rapid pace than they had been traveling earlier.

It wasn't long before they came to a fork in the road with a sign that contained the words, *Pamela's Pies*, and pointed to the left. Another sign, pointing to the right, said *Lazy W Ranch*.

"Well, I guess we know which way we want to go," exclaimed Barney.

"Which way?" asked Billy and Barney remembered the young lad could not read.

"The sign on the left," said the older man "indicates there are pies ahead! My stomach is telling me that is the way to go!"

The trail to the left wound around a curve and there in the shade of a huge boulder sat a little round house with a sign out front that said *Pamela's Pies* in dark blue lettering. On the opposite side of the road stood a tall building, somewhat strangely built in that it resembled nothing more than a large mushroom. Reaching some three stories upward with the roof of the building nestled among the branches of the tall trees; the structure had a large blue sign stretching across the front proclaiming it to be the *Blue Harness Hotel*.

The mule came to a stop and the man and boy slid to the ground. They paid scant heed to the hotel but moved instead for the doorway of *Pamela's Pies*. Just before entering, the farmer turned to the mule that stood watching them.

"This may take a little time, Two-Bits. Why don't you look around and see if you can determine just where we are?" Barney said. Then he waved to the animal and entered the pie shop.

Billy was already on a stool at the counter and Barney joined him. The cafe seemed to be empty but they could hear sounds coming from the kitchen. The farmer picked up the menu and began looking at it. From the corner of his eye, he saw the hurt look on his young friends face.

"Well, it says here that Pamela has every kind of pie known," Barney said. "I think I'll start out with a piece of good old fashioned pumpkin pie! What would you like, Billy?"

"How about cherry pie?" the youngster replied.

"That's a good choice," Barney replied, looking up as a plump smiling lady came through the doorway from the kitchen carrying a steaming fresh pie which she placed on a shelf to cool. She beamed at her two customers.

"Welcome to *Pamela's Pies*," she said with enthusiasm. "I haven't seen you fellows in here before, so you must be strangers. What can I get for you?"

Barney and Billy gave their orders and were

soon enjoying some of the best tasting pie they had ever eaten.

After the pumpkin and cherry slices, they tried raspberry cream, apricot, peach, pineapple, raisin and banana cream before pushing back from the counter.

"Wow!" said Billy. "Never have I eaten so much that was so good and made me so full! I could sure do with a nap about now!"

The waitress came to fill Barney's coffee cup and the farmer asked her politely if she might be the Pamela of *Pamela's Pies*.

"Yes, I am," she responded with a happy smile on her face. "Since I can see that you two are strangers, might I ask where you are going?"

Barney and Billy looked at each other and shrugged. "We don't know," replied the farmer. "We don't even know where we are now. I believe you could say we are lost!"

"Oh," replied Pamela, "you are in the land of the Munchkins, sometimes called Munchkin Country. You may have noticed we are a little bit partial to the color blue!"

The man and boy looked at each other and nodded. Indeed, they had noticed.

Pamela looked at Billy with a big smile on her face. "I have never seen a boy so full he could not eat a dish of ice cream," she said. "While your friend here drinks his coffee, I shall bring you a dish of the best ice cream in all of Oz!"

"Do you have chocolate?" Billy asked.

"Indeed I do," Pamela replied and disappeared into the kitchen.

A moment later, she sat a nice sized bowl of dark brown ice cream in front of young Billy. "Eat up," she said with a wink, "but don't eat quite all of it."

"Okay," said Billy picking up his spoon and dipping into the bowl. He was not sure what the woman meant about not eating it all, but he was not too concerned. After the first spoonful, he looked at Barney. "This is the best ice cream ever!" he said. "You should try some!"

Barney smiled and shook his head. "I'm too full," he said. "I'll just stick with my coffee." The farmer still had the roll of baling wire looped over his shoulder and as he relaxed over his coffee, he reached up and removed the wire, laying it beside him on the counter. He took another swallow of coffee and then began absentmindedly playing with the wire. First he rolled it and then he twisted, then he looped and pulled on the wire. After a few moments he pushed his coffee cup to one side and really got to work on his baling wire project. As his fingers were bending, pulling and straightening the wire, a figure began to take shape.

"Wow, that's a neat looking little dog," said Billy, who had stopped eating ice cream to watch his friend work. "You sure know how to work with that wire!"

"Well," replied Barney, "it's not a whole lot different than whittling a good stick of wood. It takes patience and an eye for detail," he added. He sat the finished piece on the counter top.

"What kind of dog is it?" the boy asked, looking at the figure that stood approximately six inches in height beside his bowl of ice cream.

"That's a greyhound, Billy," the farmer replied. "Lots of farmers out in western Kansas have a few greyhounds around. They use them to chase coyotes in the winter time and they make real nice pets for the kids."

"That is very nice," came the voice of Pamela. "I can see what your talent would be here in Oz, sir."

"Oh, I'm sorry," said Barney. "I just plumb forgot my manners. I'm Barnaby Fields. Most folks just call me Barney, and my pal here is Billy."

With that he reached into his bib pocket for money to pay for their food. He took the small book, *The Laughing Dragon of Oz*, out first and laid it on the counter top as he fished in the pocket for the desired bills.

"Oh," said Pamela, seeing Barney pull several greenbacks from his front pocket, "I forgot you were strangers here in Oz. No one pays for anything here. Everyone does something worthwhile and we just share. There is no need for money."

The woman had noticed the Big Little Book on the counter and she was looking at it strangely. "This is an odd Oz book," she finally said in a soft whisper, reaching out to pick up the chubby little story book. "Did you know Oz books are full of magic?" she asked.

"Well, I suppose..." Barney began and then stopped. He was in Oz! What did he really know about the Oz stories? He shook his head and then returned the bills to his bib pocket in the overalls.

"Yes," Pamela continued, "the Oz stories are

full of magic and there are times the books themselves are magic."

Neither Barney nor Billy said anything.

"Princess Ozma, years ago, decreed that there should be no more practicing magicians or sorcerers in Oz with the exception of Glinda, the Good Witch of Oz, the Wizard of Oz, and Princess Ozma of Oz. Now, there is still plenty of magic in Oz, but no one is to be casting spells and all that sort of thing!"

Barney cleared his throat. "Does that mean," He asked, "that we are in violation of some law or something by having an Oz book?"

"Oh no," Pamela laughed. "Occasionally, when the combination is right, an Oz book and some other sort of magic can combine! One never knows what will happen then!"

The waitress returned the little book to a spot on the counter beside the wire dog. Then she turned to Billy.

"How's it going with the ice cream?" she asked.

"Oh, it's really good!" replied the boy and Barney looked at the bowl with a sudden feeling of apprehension. Billy had been eating for a good while and the bowl was still just as full as it was when Pamela had set it in front of him.

The pie maker smiled at the boy and was about to return to her kitchen when she brushed against the little wire dog ever so lightly. The dog slid across the counter and collided with the bowl of ice cream. Slowly the figure of the dog tipped until his muzzle was in the ice cream.

Billy started to giggle and then stopped. He felt the hair on the back of his neck rising as he watched.

Barney, with his coffee cup halfway to his mouth, stopped and his eyes grew wide.

The waitress gasped and gripped the edge of the counter with both hands, her face growing pale.

The greyhound's tail was wagging and his jaws were working as he ate the ice cream. The little wire dog was definitely alive and seemed to be quite hungry.

Barnaby Fields regained his composure first. His eyebrows drew together and his forehead knitted in thought. He sat his cup down and shook his head slightly. Then he reached out and picked up the wire dog. The little creature turned and looked at him with soft brown eyes.

"I made this thing and I can take it apart," Barney said to himself as he began to unwind the wire.

"Wait," came a small high pitched voice. "Don't take me apart! I just got here! I'll be your good buddy!"

"If I had wanted a good buddy, I would have made a monkey or a cat!" Barney said, in a voice that was not good natured. He continued to unwind the wire dog until he had one nice long piece of wire.

"I can't eat all this ice cream," said Billy to Pamela, as Barney worked on straightening the wire.

"I know," replied the woman. "That is a magic bowl of ice cream. No one can eat it all! That's what is nice about it! You never run out!"

"Is that what made the dog come to life?" asked

Billy.

Pamela's eyes widened slightly. "I don't know," she said.

"You said there was magic in the Oz book and if it got together with another kind of magic, no one would know what the outcome would be," said Billy. "I think the two kinds of magic got together and caused the dog to come to life!"

"You may be right," the woman said. "I wonder how we would know for sure."

"I'm 'way ahead of you," said Barney. They looked over at the farmer and watched his old fingers at work on the strand of baling wire. For long minutes they watched in silence as the farmer worked.

"What are you making?" Billy finally asked.

"A monkey," replied Barney. "I said I'd rather have a monkey. Now I'm going to see if it will come to life, too!"

It was growing darker outside as heavy blue storm clouds gathered in the sky but the occupants of the cafe, *Pamela's Pies*, did not notice. A mule stood by the outside window looking through the glass at the very intently busy trio inside the building. Finally he walked over to the door and pushed with his forehead. The door swung open and Two-Bits walked inside. Just as he entered there was a crash of thunder and rain began to fall. At first it fell in a few scattered drops but gained in volume as the minutes passed.

Barnaby Fields did not notice the darkness or the thunder and lightning. He was only vaguely aware of Two-Bits looking over his shoulder.

Pamela turned on more lights in the cafe.

At last Barney placed a well-made little wire monkey on the counter and leaned back in his chair. He pushed the Oz book up beside the creature and then gently bumped the wire monkey into the ice cream. Everyone stood motionless and speechless waiting for something to happen. Nothing did.

Finally Barney let out a long sigh. "No monkey," he said as he reached over and picked the little figure out of the ice cream. He wiped the ice cream from the figure's face and then his fingers went to work quickly and it was soon obvious he was transforming the monkey into a cat.

Rain was falling in sheets outside when Barney placed the finished cat on the counter by the Oz book and tried his experiment again. The farmer, the boy, the pie maker and the mule watched breathlessly as nothing happened.

"Well, so much for that," the man said as he began unwinding the cat and putting the wire back into a roll.

"Barney," said Billy, "that seemed like an awfully nice little dog. Why don't you make him again? He might come back to life."

"Sure," said Pamela with a big smile, "try the dog again."

Barney shrugged his shoulders and began working on the wire shaping it into the form of a greyhound. It took a little time and Barney's fingers were quite tired by the time the dog was finished. He straightened up from bending over the wire sculpture and placed the figure on the counter. Immediately the tail began wagging and the head turned toward Barney.

"I'm sure glad you brought me back," the little dog said in his high pitched voice as he began bouncing around on the counter.

Billy, beaming from ear to ear, leaned toward the little fellow. "What's your name?" he asked.

The greyhound turned toward Barney. "You made me," he said, still bouncing around in his excitement. "What are you going to call me?"

"Well," said Barney, scratching his head in thought, "you're made out of wire and you keep bouncing around, so I think we'll call you Bouncer!"

CHAPTER FIVE:
THE WOOT WAGON

The Shaggy Man and the Hungry Tiger walked throughout the night on the road leading to the Land of the Winkies. It was near morning when they stopped for a short breather. They were a long way from the Royal Palace in the Emerald City of Oz, but they still had a very long distance to cover before reaching the tin castle of Nick Chopper, otherwise known as the Tin Woodman.

"You have impressed me," said the Hungry Tiger as they rested beneath a large tree in the moonlight. The Shaggy Man was munching on one of the apples he had picked up as they were leaving the Emerald City.

"Thank you," he said. "I have had much experience traveling and I can stride right along." He took another bite of his apple. "Care for an apple?" he asked, remembering his manners but forgetting that tigers generally don't eat fruit or vegetables.

The tiger rumbled deep in his throat, a sound that passed as a laugh. "Thanks, but no thanks," he said.

Dawn was just beginning to brighten the eastern sky when the Shaggy Man and the Hungry Tiger resumed their journey. They had not gone far when they heard a strange sound. It had a whirring effect and at the same time was rather squeaky.

The Shaggy Man and the Hungry Tiger looked at each other.

"What can that be?" asked the tiger.

"I don't know," replied his companion, "but I have found it is a good course of action to stay out of sight until one learns the answer." Quickly the two travelers moved off the road and hid in the heavy brush. They lay down and wriggled forward until they could see the road upon which they had been traveling.

In a short time, a strange vehicle appeared on the roadway. It was flat and had four wheels and was slightly larger than a bed. An awning was held up by four posts, one at each corner that gave protection from the heat of the sun. On the flat portion of the contraption were two benches for sitting and at the front was a single stool located behind a set of handle bars, quite like a bicycle. There was something on the bottom side of the vehicle that seemed to be causing the occasional whirring noise but the squeaky sounds were coming from the wheels.

Sitting on the driver's stool was a young man. His unruly blond hair waved in the breeze created by the swift movement of the contraption he was guiding. He appeared to be a boy in his mid-teens.

"Don't I know that young man?" said the Shaggy Man rising up so that he was on his hands and knees as he peered at the approaching vehicle.

"I wouldn't know," replied the Tiger, "but he somehow reminds me of a young fellow that spent time in the Emerald City a good while back."

"Oh, yes!" exclaimed the Shaggy Man leaping to his feet. "That is Woot! You remember Woot the Wanderer, don't you?"

"Indeed I do," replied the Hungry Tiger sagely. "I suggest you hurry out to the roadside and ask him to stop. I will wait. People sometimes do strange things when they see a tiger running toward them," he explained.

The Shaggy Man, although dressed in silks and linens and with gold lace and fancy buttons upon his apparel, still looked more like a hobo than a man of means in the Land of Oz.

When the young man looked up and saw the shaggy apparition rushing toward him, he turned his machine away and picked up speed. It was only when he heard his name being called that he looked back and recognized a former acquaintance from the Emerald City. He turned his conveyance in a circle and returned to the Shaggy Man. It was then that the Hungry Tiger arose from his position among the bushes and joined the humans on the road.

"Woot, the Wanderer!" exclaimed the Shaggy

Man as he reached out and shook hands with the young man. "It has been long since we have seen you. I trust your wandering has been going well?"

"Good morning to you, Mr. Shaggy Man," said Woot as he stepped down from his strange mode of transportation. "Yes, my travels have been going very well. Now what brings you so far from the Royal Palace of Oz?"

"We are delivering a message for Princess Ozma," replied the Shaggy Man with a small note of pride in his voice.

"Good morning to you, Hungry Tiger," said the young man as the striped beast approached.

"Good morning, Woot, my friend," the tiger replied. "Now what, may I ask, is this thing upon which you are traveling?"

"This, my friends," said Woot as he looked with pride upon the odd vehicle that somewhat resembled a bicycle, a wagon, and a bus all rolled into one, "is what I call my Spring-o-Wagon. You see, there is a large coil spring on the bottom side of the floor. I wind it each morning and the Spring-o-Wagon will carry me all day! I suppose there is some magic to it as the spring should not last all day, but with one winding, the Spring-o-Wagon does!"

"A Spring-o-Wagon, huh?" questioned the Shaggy Man. "Seems to me to be a rather long name for something I would assume you use quite often."

"Yes, the name is rather long," agreed Woot, "but I haven't come up with a better one yet. And, yes, I use the Spring-o-Wagon very much."

"Might I suggest," said the Hungry Tiger, "that you call your vehicle the Woot Wagon?"

Woot scratched his head and thought for a moment. "You are right. It would be easier to say." Then his face brightened. "If you are delivering a message of any distance, perhaps I can be of help with transportation!"

The Hungry Tiger and the Shaggy Man looked at each other. While they were both excellent travelers, perhaps riding with Woot on his Spring-o-Wagon would not be such a bad idea at that.

"We'd be happy to ride with you on your Woot Wagon," said the Hungry Tiger, "if, indeed, that was your offer."

Woot grinned. "That was my offer," he laughed. "Now just where were you fellows to deliver that message?"

"To Nick Chopper, the Tin Woodman in the land of the Winkies," answered the Shaggy Man. "The message may not be urgent, but Princess Ozma has entrusted us to deliver it and deliver it we shall!" he added with a significant bob of his shaggy head.

"I remember Nick Chopper very well," replied Woot, his eyes lighting up. "We had quite an adventure as I recall. I would be happy to make the journey to see my old friend again. Also, I would enjoy having the Hungry Tiger and the Shaggy Man accompany me. After all, the life of a wanderer is a lonely one!"

The Hungry Tiger stepped onto the 'Woot Wagon' as he called it, and lay down on the floor just in front of the last bench. The Shaggy Man likewise stepped aboard and sat down on the seat just behind the driver. Woot reached under the left edge of the vehicle and turned a key that wound the Spring-o-Wagon for the day. Then he mounted his seat and they were on their way.

Woot's mode of transportation moved rapidly along the road leading to the home of the Tin Woodman in the Winkie Country. The cool breeze caused by the speed of the Spring-o-Wagon was refreshing, especially after the sun reached midmorning. However, the canopy covering kept the riders comfortable and they talked of many things as they traveled.

"Woot," said the Shaggy Man at one point during the conversation, "in a land where no one grows old, I take it you chose to reach your present age before stopping the aging process."

Woot nodded in agreement. "Yes, I felt that I was somewhat young to be a wanderer. I believe I am much safer at this advanced age."

"Advanced age!" snorted the Shaggy Man, thinking of his own age. "You're still just a young fellow."

It was late afternoon when the Hungry Tiger raised his head from where he had been napping. His ears pricked up as he listened. Then he stood up, his head cocked to one side in a very attentive attitude.

Both Woot and the Shaggy Man took notice of their friend and the teenager brought the Woot Wagonto a stop. In the distance they could hear a whining sound mixed with sobs. It was coming from beyond a rocky slope that was also covered with brush.

"I think we should check that out," said the Hungry Tiger. "It sounds like someone in distress!"

"Sounds like caterwauling to me," put in Woot.

The Shaggy Man laughed. "I certainly don't know what to make of it," he said. "However, I agree. We need to check it out."

Woot turned his contraption toward the rock covered hill and the crying sound. Then he brought the vehicle to a halt. "I can't take the Woot Wagon up that hill," he said. "It's too rough!"

"That is all right," said the Shaggy Man. "Hungry Tiger and I need to stretch our legs. We'll just scoot over the hill and see what is going on."

"I'll wait here with the Woot Wagon," said Woot as he moved his cart into the shade of a tree. "Don't be gone too long as I am curious as to what is making all that racket!"

The Hungry Tiger stepped off the Woot Wagon and bounded up the hill, not waiting for the Shaggy Man.

"Humph!" the old fellow snorted. "Well, how do you like that?" Then he too started up the hill but at a much slower rate of speed. Presently the whining and sobbing noises stopped.

The Shaggy Man reached the crest of the hill and came to a halt. He placed his hands on his hips while the light wind played with his long hair and beard. Then he turned back towards Woot and his wagon. Coming over the hill just behind him was the Hungry Tiger and beside him bounded two young cubs.

"What are you doing with those little cubs?"

Woot called as they approached.

The Hungry Tiger just shook his head and refrained from a reply until he stood beside the Woot Wagon. Then he sat down on his haunches, licked a paw and washed his face lightly. Woot could see that it had been lightly smudged with dirt.

"My friends," said the tiger, "behold two lost cubs! They are twins, they say, and their mother just vanished while they were fishing several days ago. They are hungry and I have promised that we would find them nourishment."

Woot scratched his left ear but said nothing. Before him were the cub of a grizzly bear and the cub of a leopard.

The Shaggy Man pursed his lips as if he were about to whistle, but did not. He simply nodded his head and twisted his beard thoughtfully.

"All aboard," said Woot. "Let's hit the road and find a snack for the little ones." They all loaded onto the Woot Wagon and the young wanderer guided it down the road in the direction of Winkie Country.

In a short while the little bear's nose began to twitch and soon he was snuffling around the fancy clothing worn by the Shaggy Man. The fellow watched him closely and soon the little bear cub began trying to chew on the man's pant leg.

"Oh, you want an apple!" exclaimed the Shaggy Man. He reached into his pocket and produced a shiny red apple which he split in half with his pocket knife and then handed to the cub. The bear began to chew greedily on the morsel. The little leopard cub just lay curled up by the Hungry Tiger and looked forlorn, for leopards do not eat apples.

"See that house off the road a ways to the south?" asked the Shaggy Man a short time later. "I suggest we drive over there and see if there is any milk or other food we can obtain for our little friends."

Woot immediately turned the Woot Wagon in the direction of the farm house. He maneuvered his vehicle down a pleasant lane lined with blooming lilac bushes and came to a stop before a front porch. The Shaggy Man immediately hopped off the wagon and went to the door.

Upon his knock, a matronly lady appeared. She was holding a large spoon in one hand and a mixing bowl in the crook of her arm.

"Begging your pardon," the man said. "We were wondering if we could get some food for our little cubs as they are very hungry."

"Yes indeed," the lady beamed. "You just sit tight and I will be right out with the fish and milk! Perhaps I can even spare a few cookies," and she laughed as though she had told a joke.

She was as good as her word and in a few moments the occupants of the Woot Wagon were feasting on fish, milk and a large platter of fresh cookies. The little cubs, whose names were Trixie and Moxie, were soon curled up asleep by the Hungry Tiger, their tummies filled with food.

The Shaggy Man thanked the woman kindly and promised to stop for a visit someday when her husband was at home. Then the travelers were on their way again.

CHAPTER SIX:
RIDERS OF THE BLUE SAGE

They stood in *Pamela's Pies* and watched the rain falling in torrents from the dark sky. Billy was holding Bouncer in his arms and Barney was replacing *The Laughing Dragon of Oz* in his bib pocket. The mule had folded his knees and lay down on the floor near the door. Pamela stood with her arms crossed, gazing through the plate glass window at the falling rain.

"Doesn't look like you fellows will be going very far," she commented, "unless you want to get soaked."

"Yeah," agreed the farmer. "Looks like we need to look for a dry place to spend the night."

"Try across the street," suggested Pamela. "Old Clem runs the *Blue Harness Hotel* and that is what his business is, putting people up for the night!"

"We'll do that," laughed Barney. "I don't suppose you'd mind if we just waited here until that rain lets up?"

"Not at all," the pie maker replied. "And remember," She added, "there is no charge for staying in the hotel."

A short time later Pamela reappeared from her kitchen with a box of dominoes which she placed on a table. Then she placed a cloth sack beside it. The printing on the side read *'Pamela's Pies.'*

"I brought something for you," the woman said, looking at Barney. "You have in your pocket a book, a magical book, it seems. You're taking a big chance of having the book destroyed just carrying it around like that! So, I have brought you a little box that looks as if it were just made to carry your book." She reached into the sack and brought out a small box that glimmered and shone in the light of the cafe.

"Gold!" exclaimed Billy. He reached out and Pamela let him take the box in his hands. He turned it over slowly and gently rubbed the glowing container.

"No, it's not gold, Billy," she said. "It is gold plated so it looks like gold. Now, see if you can figure out how to open it!"

Billy turned the box over carefully looking for the lid. There did not seem to be one. There was scroll work on each of the four sides and the top and bottom. There was no sign of hinges, nor was there a clasp.

"I can't even tell which side is up," the boy finally said.

"Let me show you," said Pamela. She took the box and turned it. "See this engraving," she said, indicating the scroll work. "You turn it so these marks are on the top, like this," she turned the box, showing them how to hold it. "Then you have it right side up. The trick to opening the box is to hold it level, then place your fingers and thumbs like so. Then push on the lower corners with your bottom fingers and...." The box lid popped open.

Barney took the box, held it just right and with the right pressure, the lid popped up. "Bingo!" exclaimed Billy. "Let me try it." It took the boy several tries before he could get it to work.

"Now," said Pamela, "let's see if *The Laughing Dragon of Oz* will fit into the box."

Barney reached into his bib pocket and produced the book, which he handed to the woman. Carefully she slipped the little book into the gold plated box and snapped the lid shut. The fit was nearly perfect.

"There it is," she said, "safe and sound, and the box is waterproof too."

Barney then practiced with the box until he caught the knack of opening it easily. Pamela replaced the box containing the book in the small sack and handed it to Barney. The farmer thanked her kindly for her generosity and started to reach for his bib pocket. Then he thought better of offering to pay for the box.

The rain continued for the remainder of the day and Barney, Billy, Two-Bits, and Bouncer sat at a table near the window and played dominoes through most of the afternoon. In the early evening they saw a rider stop at the hotel and dismount, taking his riding animal inside with him.

"Was that a horse?" asked Barney. "It sure didn't look like one! I wonder what it was?" He continued looking out the window through the rain toward the building across the street.

"No, it wasn't a horse or a mule," replied Two-Bits. He did not elaborate and Barney assumed he didn't know what it was.

It was near nightfall when the rain dwindled to a light sprinkle. Barney and his friends bid good-bye to Pamela and crossed the street to the hotel. The bottom floor of the building was the stable and where Two-Bits would spend the night.

Clem, the proprietor, met them at the door and welcomed them to the *Blue Harness Hotel*. He gave a wave of his arm toward the stable area and told Two-Bits to find a stall that suited him and if he needed more straw, to just let him know. The mule thanked the man and wandered back into the stable area.

"Now, boys," said Clem, an elderly man with a white handle bar mustache and wearing a black wide brimmed western style hat, "let me show you to your room."

The sun was just lighting the eastern sky the next morning when Barney and Billy, carrying Bouncer in his arms, came down the stairs. Old Clem sat in a wooden chair leaned back against the wall near the stable door.

"Morning, boys," he called. "Going to get an early start, are you?"

"We thought we might," replied Barney. "We'll

see if Two-Bits is agreeable."

"That other fellow left about an hour ago. I thought that was pretty early. It was still dark out when he saddled his razorback and hit the road," Clem said, shaking his head.

"Razorback!" exclaimed Barney. "Did you say razorback? Like a razorback hog?"

"Oh, yeah," replied Clem knowingly. He let his chair down and stood up. "All them fellas out at the Lazy W ride razorbacks. Mean looking critters, too!"

"I just never heard of such a thing," replied Barney. "Wouldn't that be kind of hard to do? Ride a razorback, I mean."

"Well, I expect so," Clem replied. "But these fellas have special saddles which makes it somewhat easier. They also feed the hogs on those blue pickles to kind of keep their nasty disposition under control. Those tuskers can get downright mean when they haven't had their pickles!"

Barney was confused and just stood there, shaking his head slowly.

"Where are you boys off to this morning?" Clem was asking. The farmer made no reply as he tried to sort everything out.

"We are looking for a man known as the Prankster," came Two-Bits' deep voice. "Do you know who I'm talking about?"

"Well, yeah, I've heard of that guy," replied Clem. "But I've never seen him. Don't know that he's in these parts."

"Neither do we," replied Two-Bits. "We're just trying to pick up his trail."

"Well," said Clem, scratching his head, "I think I'd go check with the boss of the O-Bar-Z Ranch. They usually have a good line on what's going on."

"I guess that's where we'll go then," responded Barney.

"Say," said Clem, "I noticed when you boys rode in here yesterday, that you didn't have a saddle. Would you like one? I've got an extra in the tack room."

"Sure," replied Barney, thinking how much more comfortable it would be in a saddle than riding bareback. And Barney was beginning to get the hang of not paying for anything.

A short time later, Barney and Billy, with the boy still holding Bouncer, were in the saddle and heading down the road at a fairly good clip.

Several hours passed as the morning sun rose higher in the sky. Barney and Billy rode Two-Bits at a steady pace along the road. The trees remained tall and cast a great deal of shade over their way. Growing beside the road and in the sometimes visible ditches were various species of flowers. Many of them were familiar varieties to Barney but others were not. Most of them, although not all, were of some shade of blue. Many of them were purple or lavender. There were a few wild roses along the way and those were a deep red with seemingly no tinge of blue in their coloring. The same was true with the tall sunflower plants, their blossoms being a deep beautiful yellow.

"Barney," said Billy, who was sitting behind the farmer with his arms wrapped around his waist, "I sure could use some of Pamela's pies about now."

"So could I," Barney laughed. "Last night, I thought I'd never want to eat another pie!" He looked up at the sun and commented, "It is about noon, Billy."

A strange snorting noise came from the bushes beside the road and Two-Bits suddenly burst into top speed as he raced down the road. Barney was hard put to stay in the saddle. The mule's ears were laid back against his head and he was fairly flying, he was running so fast. Then Barney heard noises behind them and looked back.

"What," he exclaimed, "are those?"

Following them were three razorback hogs carrying riders that resembled nothing less than large frogs dressed in western garb. The creatures were a mottled green in color with flat looking faces containing a wide mouth and bulging eyes. They wore chaps and boots with spurs and sat in strange looking contraptions that had to be saddles specifically made to fit the razorbacks they were riding.

The hogs, although somewhat short legged were extremely large coming up to near shoulder level with Two-Bits. They ran with a peculiar bounding gait that made it look extremely hard for the riders to stay mounted. Their heads were held low to the ground and from the sides of their mouths; they sported a set of wicked looking ivory tusks. Their small eyes seemed to glimmer redly, however, Barney wasn't sure but what the color was his imagination.

Two-Bits had been traveling all morning with Barney and Billy on his back and he did not have the energy to hold out for long against the big hogs following him. Gradually he began slowing, his breath coming in labored gasps.

Shortly the weird looking riders were galloping along on either side of the straining mule. Slower and slower came Two-Bits' strides. Finally in exasperation, he came to a halt. The mule stood with his head down, wheezing from the exertion.

Barney and Billy sat on Two-Bits' back and stared at the strange riders, speechless for the moment. The riders mounted on the razorbacks returned the stares. Finally, Barney cleared his throat and spoke.

"Why are you chasing us?" he asked, looking from one to the other of the three creatures.

"You are on the range of the Lazy W," came the hissing reply from one of the frog-like riders. "We shall take you to the boss and see what we should do with you."

"Just where is this boss?" Barney asked.

One of the greenish looking riders raised a long slim arm and pointed across the undulating plain toward a distant plateau just visible through the bluish haze that surrounded it.

"Move," said one of the riders, pointing again in the direction of the Lazy W headquarters. Two-Bits turned and started toward the plateau.

Barney realized the sage brush they were passing through had a deep blue tinge to the silver colored leaves and even the gray stems and branches contained a smattering of blue. Two-Bits was feeling the fatigue and set a rather slow pace which seemed to upset the riders of the razorbacks but they could also tell the mule was quite tired.

An hour's riding put them at the foot of the sloping side of the plateau and they turned onto a trail that switch backed its way to the top. The path was steep in places and Barney and Billy got off the mule's back to make it easier for him to climb. It was at this point the razorback riders noticed the small bag fastened to the mule's saddle.

"What is in the sack?" one of the fellows asked.

"Oh, just some personal belongings," replied Barney in a matter-of-fact voice. He tried to give the impression that it contained nothing of importance. It almost worked. They continued up the trail for several minutes before coming to a level spot. Here the captors allowed them to stop for a brief rest before continuing onward.

"Let me see the sack," said one of the green men reaching for the small bag hanging from the saddle. Barney started to protest and then thought better of the action.

"I'm a farmer," said Barney trying to distract their attention from the sack. "What are you fellows?"

"We are ranch hands on the Lazy W," replied one of the riders. "We are the best muddlumps to ever ride this range!"

The first creature had removed the small sack and pulled open the drawstring. His eyes lit up and he closed the bag immediately.

"Nothing much here," the muddlump said, fastening the bag to his own belt, but his companions had seen his initial reaction.

"Reckon I'd like to take a look in that bag!"

declared the one standing closest to the fellow with the bag. He reached out to take the sack, but his partner immediately moved out of reach. The third muddlump stepped forward quickly.

"Must be something important in there," he said. "In which case, we must turn it over to Bobcat Bob up at the ranch house."

The first muddlump wilted slightly as he realized he would not be allowed to keep the gold box in the bag. With a shrug, he handed the small sack to his companions. They hissed deeply in surprise at the golden container. Quickly they removed it from the sack and began searching for a way to open it.

Without thinking, Billy started to move toward the muddlumps to show them how to get the box open but Barney caught him by the shoulder and signaled silence with one finger to his lips.

"It's better if they don't know how to get it open," the farmer whispered.

The three Lazy W hands spent considerable time trying to figure out how the box worked. Not once did they think of asking the man or the boy to show them. Finally, in evident disgust, they resumed their march up the trail toward the top of the plateau.

A short while later they reached the summit and it was just a short jaunt to the sprawling log ranch house. Bobcat Bob, the owner of the Lazy W, was not around when the muddlumps arrived with their prisoners. After a long discussion, they decided to leave the golden box on the dining room table.

Barney, Billy, and Two-Bits were taken to the

large barn just a short distance from the house. The mule was tethered in a stall on the lower level while Barney and Billy were taken upstairs to the hayloft. They were bound hand and foot and left on the hay to await the coming of Bobcat Bob.

"Say," called Barney, as the frog-like muddlumps were ready to descend the steps. "What is your boss like? What can we expect from him?" Previous attempts at conversation had failed and the farmer was somewhat surprised when the creatures threw back their heads and gave a loud hissing sound. He assumed they were laughing in their way.

One of the muddlumps walked halfway back to the bound prisoners while the other two waited by the stairs. "Old Bob is downright mean," was the fellows reply. "He has a mine back in the hills and any stranger found on the Lazy W range ends up working in the mine."

"For how long?" asked Barney.

"Forever," came the reply, as the three muddlumps gave their strange hissing laugh and turned to descend the stairs.

"Golly, Barney, what do we do now?" asked Billy in a low voice when he was sure the muddlumps had left the barn.

"I don't know," replied the old farmer with a shake of his head. "I don't recall ever being tied up in a hayloft before!" About that time Barney felt a movement in his pocket and out climbed the wire dog, Bouncer.

"Bouncer!" exclaimed Billy. "I'd forgotten all about you!"

The little greyhound was bouncing around on

the loft floor with his tail wagging so hard the farmer wondered if he would build up enough heat to break the wire.

"Do you suppose you could chew through these ropes, Bouncer?" the boy asked.

The little dog's eyes sparkled and Billy noticed he was looking more and more like a real dog and less and less like a wire dog.

"You just watch," was the pup's reply as he set to work on the bonds. It didn't take the little fellow very long as his wire teeth seemed to be very sharp. In just moments, Billy was untying the knots at his ankles.

"Well," said Barney, as Billy loosened the ropes around his wrists, "if I had any reservations about making the little dog before, they are all gone now!"

The little greyhound bounded onto the farmer's lap and stretched as high as he could to lick the man's chin.

Two-Bits registered surprise when he saw the man and boy, who was carrying the little wire dog, coming down the steps from the hay loft. The farmer unsnapped the tether rope and led the mule to the saddle.

"I've got an idea," said Two-Bits. "I think you know how tired I was out there this afternoon, so why don't you just saddle up two of those hogs and ride them? It sure would help me out!"

"Good idea," said the farmer, moving over to the area when the hogs were grunting and eating on a pile of blue pickles. "I wonder which ones are the fastest," he said as he looked over the herd.

One of the hogs raised his head, slobbers and

blue pickle juice running out of his mouth as he munched on the food. "The fast ones," he said with a little smirk on his wart covered face, "are the ones over there with their own eating troughs!"

Barney turned and looked in the direction indicated by the razorback. Sure enough, there were several animals that had separate stalls against the right wall. They, too, were munching away on the blue pickles.

Then Barney noticed several strange looking beasts against the wall at the far end and wondered if they were faster than the hogs. At that moment one turned and looked at him and Barney decided he wanted nothing to do with the creature. The face had been that of a giant lizard with a black tongue flicking in and out of his mouth.

Since the animals were well fed, they were quite docile. Barney and Billy had no trouble in getting the strange contraptions known as razorback saddles strapped onto their backs. In a few minutes they were ready to go.

They moved to the barn door and looked outside. Shadows were getting long as the evening approached. They noticed the light was on in the ranch house and that reminded them of the little gold box and the magic book.

"I suppose we should make an attempt to get our box back," Barney remarked.

"If it can be accomplished without jeopardizing our safety, then I say we should make the attempt," offered the mule. "But if we are going to run afoul of these muddlumps again, then I say forget it."

"Mr. Barney," said Billy, in a somewhat bashful

tone, "this falls into an area where I have some experience. Please let me see what I can do about retrieving the book."

The farmer looked the boy over carefully and decided the youngster probably had some experience in deftly taking things. He nodded.

"You be careful," he said. "Don't take any chances and we'll wait for you right here in the shadows of the barn."

Billy grinned and slipped away. The little wire dog followed quietly at his heels.

CHAPTER SEVEN:
THE MARSH MONSTER

The occupants of the Woot Wagon, as the Hungry Tiger called the rolling contraption, could see the shining tin turrets of the Nick Chopper's castle long before they reached it.

As they rolled to a stop in front of the castle they were met by a Winkie guard, smartly outfitted in armor of tin mail. The polished metal of his garment twinkled and shone as he moved. He recognized the Hungry Tiger and the Shaggy Man immediately and promptly went to inform his emperor that the famous personages from the Emerald City were here.

The Tin Woodman was overjoyed to see his old friends, including Woot the Wanderer. When he was informed they were bearing a message from Princess Ozma, the emperor immediately declared that a feast would be held in honor of the occasion. Food was immediately prepared and since the travelers were quite hungry, they did not mind that the message should wait.

The Hungry Tiger took his two little cubs to the stables where they were treated royally. They were also quite a hit with the other beasts of the barn although no one was quite sure how the twin bit worked.

Later as the banquet was winding down, the Shaggy Man stood up and announced that he and the Hungry Tiger had been sent by Princess Ozma with a message concerning Captain Fyter. He explained that the good Captain was bound hand and foot somewhere up in the Gillikin Country but that he was quite capable of taking care of himself. He then explained that Princess Ozma was leaving the decision to the Emperor of the Winkie Country concerning any rescue effort. Some discussion was in order as to whether the good Captain would be all right if left to his own devices or if a contingent should be sent to his rescue.

At length and leaving nothing to chance, they decided that someone should check out the situation. The Tin Woodman stood up before his assembled guests and said that he would be pleased to go as he and Captain Fyter, the only other tin man in Oz, were the next thing to being brothers.

Woot, being a wanderer of the highest rank, volunteered to accompany his old friend and contribute the services of his Woot Wagon as the vehicle was now being called.

The Shaggy Man immediately consented to go

with them, allowing as how this excursion had adventure written all over it.

But when the Hungry Tiger heard of the plans, he respectfully declined to go as he now had the obligation of caring for the twin cubs. His immediate plans were to take the cubs back to the Emerald City and when Princess Ozma returned, ask her to check the Magic Picture to locate the mother of the cubs. Then it would be up to the Hungry Tiger to see that the little ones were returned to their proper place.

The Tin Woodman was ready to leave immediately in the search for Captain Fyter but both Woot and the Shaggy Man insisted they sleep the remainder of the night before embarking on their new adventure. The emperor, who needed no sleep because he was not a meat and bone person, agreed that his friends should get their rest before they started.

The rising sun was just edging above the horizon when the Shaggy Man and Woot finished the excellent breakfast provided for them by Nick Chopper. When they had finished the meal, they immediately went to the stables where the Woot Wagon had been housed overnight. Saying goodbye to the Hungry Tiger, they boarded the vehicle and soon the tin city surrounding the tin castle was left far behind.

They traveled north expecting to reach the Gillikin Country in a day's ride on the Woot Wagon. The teenage wanderer explained that he seldom rolled the vehicle as fast as it would go because he did not get to enjoy the country in the manner he wished. Therefore, in his own travels, he moved at a more moderate rate of speed. Now, however, he let the coil spring push the wagon at a fairly rapid clip.

The first day was uneventful, although they traveled through country none of them had visited previously. The Magical Kingdom of Oz was large indeed!

On the morning of the second day, they came upon a narrow road that was going in a northerly direction and decided to follow it, at least for a time. It was packed and hard and the Woot Wagon made good time.

"My friends," observed the Shaggy Man after they had been traveling the road for a good while, "I wonder why it is, with a highway so well suited for travel, that we have met no other travelers."

Neither Woot nor the Tin Man could offer an explanation, although they did agree that it seemed a bit strange. In a short time they saw a small sign by the side of the road. The boy slowed the Woot Wagon. The sign read: *Ahead Lays the Miracle of Muddy Mire! A Marsh with a Heart!*

"That doesn't make any sense," said the Shaggy Man as they rode on toward the north and the Gillikin Country.

"Perhaps the answer lies ahead," said Woot as he began slowing the vehicle again. "The road appears to come to an end."

Presently they came to a stop and the road did seem to come to an end. Ahead of them lay a lowland area that was perhaps five or six hundred paces across. The ground level dropped ten to fifteen feet and then seemed to level out as it crossed the area. The opposite side seemed to slope upwards to regain ground level.

There was a strong smell of stale mud and water but very little of it was visible and that seemed to be off to one side of the area where the road would have crossed. Most of the area was covered with coarse grass and other types of vegetation one might find in a lowland or marshy area.

"I believe the road continues on the opposite side," said the Shaggy Man as he shaded his eyes and looked across the swampy spot.

"It seems that you are right," agreed the Tin Man. "Do you think the Woot Wagon could make it over that area out there?" he asked, addressing Woot.

The boy shrugged his shoulders. "I don't know, but we can try. The wagon is light and we can get off and carry it if we should become mired in the muck."

With that they started the Woot Wagon down the incline toward the marshy looking swamp area. The closer they got, the worse the area appeared to be. The grass was coarse and rough to drive through and the stench of stale muck was almost unbearable.

"Pick up speed," suggested the Shaggy Man. "Go as fast as you can!"

Woot did as was suggested and they raced full tilt into the stale marsh. Then they began to feel the vehicle sinking into the morass as they advanced. Woot tried to turn the front wheels to take them back the way they came. But the turned wheels just scooted up piles of mud and they were soon at a standstill.

"Time to unload and carry the wagon," said Woot, hopping off the vehicle.

"Oh, my," said the Tin Man. "This is not good. Mud and water do not work with my joints. If I should rust up," he said, "you both know where my oil can is. It is a special can which Princess Ozma fixed for me and it will not run out of oil."

By the time they had positioned themselves and were ready to lift the Woot Wagon, the vehicle had sunk to the level of the bed. The coil spring on the bottom was immersed in the muck.

They heaved and strained before they were finally able to pull the machine free of the sucking mud. Slowly they began moving toward the opposite side. They were almost half way across when the Tin Man's leg joints began moving slower and slower.

"Oh, my!" he exclaimed. "It's happening! My joints are becoming stiff!"

"Get on the wagon," replied the Shaggy Man, "before it's too late! Woot and I will carry you, too!"

The Tin Man did as he was told and while his legs had ceased to work altogether, he was able to pull himself aboard with his arms as they had not absorbed enough moisture to stiffen up.

As they continued working with the Woot Wagon, they failed to notice the swamp area directly to their left. That bit of the marsh seemed to undulate and ripple slightly. Then it moved a little and rippled some more, moving ever closer to the travelers.

Suddenly there was a very loud sucking noise as the swamp directly beside them seemed to rear up into the air. Then muddy, sloppy looking appendages reached out and slapped themselves about both Woot and the Shaggy Man. There was enough force in the maneuver that both the man and boy were knocked away from the Woot Wagon. While the vehicle began to settle back into the ooze, the Shaggy Man and Woot were lifted several feet into the air.

"Wha... what's going on?" stammered Woot.

The Shaggy Man gave a despairing whistle. "I certainly don't know," he replied in a harsh whisper. "I think maybe something has trapped us."

Both the man and the boy were slowly turned to face the marsh area and then the whole thing rose up slightly and there was a sound like distant thunder coming from the bottom side of the raised muck and goo. The rumbling slowly became a voice, speaking the language of all Ozians.

"Trespassers!" it said. "You have returned to steal what little water I have left!"

"I beg to differ," said the Shaggy Man in a weak, but determined voice. "We have never been here before now and we certainly don't want what little water you might have left."

"The last human, the one known as the Prankster, also said he did not want my water. Then when he left, he turned my marsh into a dry flat!" the voice said emphatically. "I shall never believe another human!"

"Woot," called the Shaggy Man, "are you getting drier?"

"Yes," replied the boy, "my mouth and throat are parched! I need a drink badly!"

"This thing, this marsh monster," answered the Shaggy Man, "is pulling the liquid right out of our bodies! It's absorbing our body fluids! In a few minutes we'll be completely dehydrated!"

Woot opened his mouth to reply but only a dry rasping hiss came out.

"Mr. Marsh Monster," came the voice of the Tin Man on the bed of the Woot Wagon, "let my friends go and we will see to it that water is returned to your swamp!"

"I do not believe you," replied the voice from the mire. "That Prankster thought it was funny to leave me without water. If I let you go, you will think the same!"

"Oh, look!" exclaimed the Tin Man. "Water Buffalo, at the far end of the marsh!"

Suddenly the marsh creature dropped the two humans and began a movement that resembled rippling water as it moved away.

"Quick," whispered the Tin Man, "get up and get this contraption up to drier ground."

The Shaggy Man and Woot needed no further urging. Half groggy from their sudden loss of water, they struggled to their feet and began tugging on the Woot Wagon.

"He's coming back!" shouted the Tin Man. Fear gave the teenager and the ragged appearing man abnormal strength and, hoisting the cart shoulder high, they ran toward the far edge of the marsh. They easily outdistanced the rolling monster from the mire.

Soon they were sitting on the upper edge of the road, out of reach of the monster. Both of the humans were panting and in dire need of water to replace their body liquids. The rolling muck and dry slime came to a stop some fifteen feet below them.

"I am sorry to have misled you," called the Tin Man to the rippling monster below them. "However, it was not my friends who stole your water. If, by chance, we can do something to help you get water we will do so."

There came a sound like the distant booming of thunder, but neither Woot nor the Shaggy Man could make any sense of it. The Tin Man, however, replied.

"We would be your friends if we could," he answered. "However, first things first. We must have water to replace that which you took from my friends. Next, I must get my joints working. Then we will see what can be done for you." There came another distant rumbling from the monster.

The Tin Man, sitting on the Woot Wagon because his leg joints had become stiff, turned to Woot and the Shaggy Man. "Our friend, the Marsh Monster, says there is a stream a short distance from here with good water for drinking. He says to ask the stream for water and then to let the stream know of his plight."

The Tin Man turned back to the monster and waved a tin arm. Woot went to his position on the stool before the handles and sat down.

"Is everybody ready?" he asked in a scratchy voice.

"Yes," replied the Tin Man and the Shaggy Man

nodded.

Woot applied pressure to the handle bars and nothing happened. He tried again with the same results.

"What is wrong?" gasped the older man.

"Do you need to wind the coil spring?" asked the Tin Man.

Woot sluggishly got down and tried to wind the spring. He could not turn the key. He sat down on the ground in despair.

"What is it?" asked the Tin Man.

"I think," said Woot slowly, "that our spring is full of mud. It will have to be cleaned out before it can work and we need water to do that. I think we are lost. Neither I nor Shaggy Man can make it anywhere, especially not to the creek."

"Quickly," said the Tin Man, "oil my joints so that I can begin to move. Then I can take care of things."

Woot slowly got the magic oil can and began squirting the ankle joints, the knee joints and the hip joints of the Tin Man. In a very short time, the fellow was moving and the more he moved the more fluid he became until he was as good as new.

"I shall go to the creek," he announced, "and I will soon return with water for you." So saying, the Tin Man lifted his ever-present ax and strode away.

In short order, the Emperor of the Winkie Country was back and in his hands he carried a large leaf folded in such a way as to hold water. The Shaggy Man and Woot the Wanderer drank the life giving water slowly. Gradually they could feel their strength returning and life flowing through their bodies.

At the end of an hour's time, they shouldered the Woot Wagon and carried it the distance to the creek. Once there, they turned the vehicle up on its side and Woot prepared to go into the stream to splash water on the muddy spring.

"Wait, my friends," said the Tin Man. "This is a magical creek and will do our bidding if we ask nicely."

Woot and the Shaggy Man both looked at the Tin Man in surprise.

"My friend, the creek," said the Tin Man without further ado, "please wash the underside of our Woot Wagon which is covered with mud from the marsh."

To the surprise of the man and boy, the water from the bubbling, churning creek rose into the air and began to splash on the coil spring. In moments it was clean and as shiny as the Tin Man. Then the water receded into the bed of the creek again.

"One more favor, my friend," said the Tin Man to the creek as Woot and the Shaggy Man replaced the wagon on it wheels. "Could you possibly run some water over to the marsh? It has very nearly dried up and the monster is in dire need of liquid. He believes you would help him."

As the three travelers watched, the creek changed its course and began moving in the direction of the marsh.

"Well," said the Tin Man, "I believe we have kept our word."

In a few moments, they were aboard the Woot Wagon and the young boy had the vehicle rolling along the road to the north. They were all feeling better by the moment and the cool breeze blowing in their faces felt quite good.

"You know," said the Shaggy Man as they rolled along, "I wonder what that Marsh Monster meant about a Prankster stealing his water?"

CHAPTER EIGHT:
THE PRANKSTER AT LAST!

A tall lean man walked with a rapid gait across the meadowland, following a barely discernible road that led in a winding route toward the distant hills that had a purple tint to their coloring. There was a scowl on the fellow's face and at times he strode along with his hands clasped behind his back, giving the impression, had there been anyone to notice, of being in deep thought.

His dark eyes were narrowed and his forehead furrowed giving one the feeling the man was struggling with some hidden problem. Occasionally his mouth would open and several mumbled, unintelligible words would be uttered. The corners of his thin lipped mouth were turned down. His skin was browned like that of a farmer or rancher who spends a great deal of time out of doors.

A long frock coat and black in color, hung from the narrow shoulders to almost knee length. However, the pockets were trimmed in gold cloth and the buttons down the front and on the cuffs were of a matching golden color. With pockets that appeared to be full, the unbuttoned coat swung and flopped in rhythm with the fellow's stride.

The hair on the man's head was cropped short on the top but the sides grew long and he had the long hair tied in short braids that stopped at the base of his neck. He also wore a flowing mustache that streamed backwards toward the braids as he walked.

"Well, Tommy," he muttered, speaking to himself, "those hills and the forests seem to be a might bit closer." He had stopped at the crest of a long hill and he leaned on the walking stick he carried in his right hand. His left hand reached under the heavy black coat and unhooked a water canteen from a wide, black belt that was fastened with an ornate golden buckle. He drank deeply from the container and then replaced it on the belt.

"Legs," he said, speaking aloud, "you must get moving if we are to reach our destination by nightfall." He gave a short sardonic laugh.

Again he was striding along the old and little used road. All day he walked, only pausing now and then for a drink from the canteen.

By sundown the man was in the hills, quite rocky and covered with a scattered growth of evergreen trees. He was searching for a suitable place for his evening camp when he came to a drop off at the edge of the road. He stood on the rim of a small canyon and looked downward. He nodded his head and pursed his thin lips. Then a low, evil laugh escaped his throat.

"Looks like a small cave down yonder, Tommy," he said. "Just make your way down the side of the rocky slope and you will have a nice place for the night. Out of the wind," he added, "and out of any rain. A traveler could get used to being pampered like that."

The man tucked his walking stick under his arm and lifted his coat. Then he stepped carefully over the edge and began working his way toward the bottom of the canyon and the nearby cave. It was not a deep canyon and the man did not expect to take long in reaching the bottom. He was, however, careful in working his way down the slope. However, there are things one cannot determine ahead of time, regardless of the care taken. He was now using the walking stick to steady his way, when a rock moved under the stick and the man lost his balance.

With a startled cry, the fellow fell forward and commenced rolling down the slope. He landed in a heap at the bottom, his big black coat covering him like a tablecloth. For long moments he lay still. Finally an anguished groan came from the pile. After some time, the coat was pushed back and the man rolled over, his face grimacing with pain.

"E'gads, Tommy," he gritted between clenched teeth, "I think you broke your leg! Now that's a find how-do-you-do!"

He pulled himself into a sitting position, amid obvious pain, where he remained for some period of time. He drank from his canteen and then pulled a cloth from his pocket and wiped his perspiring face.

"Got to get to that cave," he finally said. Gradually he began scooting backwards, in his sitting position, toward the mouth of the cave. Inch by tortured inch, the lean man covered the distance. His leg was swollen and purple in color and it throbbed very painfully both above and below the knee joint. Perspiration rolled down the injured fellow's face, soaking his shirt.

At last he made it to the cave at the foot of the rocky wall. It was not large and it appeared to have been occupied recently, probably by some beast of the wild. He rested a bit and drank some more from the canteen realizing it was getting close to empty and he must conserve water. He also felt he should start a fire to deter any beast that might also be planning to curl up in the cave for the night. There were a number of small sticks and twigs within his reach and the injured man managed to get a small fire going. He decided his leg was becoming somewhat numb as he didn't think he was feeling the pain as intensely now.

He pulled himself a little farther into the shelter and lay back with a moan. He closed his eyes and wiped the perspiration from his face. Then he forced himself up on one elbow and fished around in one of the large pockets of his coat until he found what he wanted. He pulled forth a thick book bound in brown leather. Carefully he opened it and paged through it by the gloom of the firelight. Finally he shook his head and laid back, his eyes closed in pain. The book lay by his side. There had been no answer inside, no spell for fixing a broken leg.

The fire caught a new twig and blazed up for a moment, illuminating the cover of the volume lying beside the man. The title read, *The Prankster's Book of Phine Pranks*.

The man lay still and quiet as the moon rose in the night sky. The fire burned down and then went out. A large animal, a burly brown bear, stopped and sniffed at the entrance of the cave, but sensing the man and the burned fire, it moved onward in the night. The man was unaware of any of these things.

In the man's semiconscious mind, there came a clap that sounded like thunder being belted out in cadence and then a voice came to him. At first he could not make out what was being said, but eventually his mind began to sort it out.

"Tommy," the voice was saying, "you have found the great book of the Prankster and you have used it for your own enjoyment and entertainment at the great expense of those coming in contact with you! Perhaps the powers that be have seen fit to pull a prank on you with the broken leg. After all, that is about as hilarious as the pranks you have been casting over the inhabitants you have chanced to meet in Oz!" Again, there came the clapping like distant thunder and Tommy felt the voice was laughing at him.

Tommy, the Prankster, realized he could be trapped here in this small canyon forever, since inhabitants of Oz never die a natural death. Trapped here, pining away of thirst and hunger and suffering untold pain for eternity was not a funny thought.

"Help me!" the man pleaded.

"Have you helped any of those on whom you

have pulled a prank? Have you released even one?" came the thunderous voice.

"No, but I will. I promise!" the man replied. "I will free everyone!"

"Perhaps I should help you," came the voice, "especially since you have promised to release everyone! Perhaps I shall cause someone to find you, but what a good prank it would be for you to suffer for a while first! Just like the victims of your pranks!" The thundering laugh faded into the distance and the voice was gone.

In the silence that followed, the Prankster wondered if he had really been conversing with some deity or if it were just a figment of his fevered imagination.

***

In the meantime, Woot the Wanderer and his two companions, the Shaggy Man and the Tin Woodman, continued riding the Woot Wagon into the interior of the Gillikin Country in search of Captain Fyter. Princess Ozma had said, in her brief instructions before leaving for her visit with Glinda the Good, that the Magic Picture had been too dark to tell exactly where the good captain was located. However, she did say that when she had previously checked on the tin soldier's whereabouts, he had been far up in the northeast portion of the Gillikin Country. Since Captain Fyter's mode of transportation was walking, he should still be somewhere in that area.

Woot and his friends were rolling rapidly in that direction. They skirted mountains and lakes. They avoided thick forests through which the vehicle could not traverse. At times there were roads to follow and at other times they simply followed the stars. Woot, the Shaggy Man and the Tin Woodman were enjoying themselves to the fullest as the days rolled by.

***

The Hungry Tiger, with Trixie and Moxie in his care, had arrived at the Emerald City. Everyone who saw the little cubs thought they were the cutest things but no one could figure out how they could be twins.

Eventually Princess Ozma arrived back in the Emerald City and the Hungry Tiger requested a conference with Her Royal Highness at her earliest possible convenience. In short order, he was granted an audience and appeared before the girl ruler with his two cubs.

"How darling!" she exclaimed as she rubbed the furry necks of each of the youngsters.

"They are twins," the Hungry Tiger stated bluntly.

"How can that be?" asked Ozma. "One is a bear cub and the other is a leopard cub. It is impossible for them to be twins."

The Hungry Tiger nodded his shaggy head. "That is my problem," he said. "I have promised I would help them return to their mother. However, I do not know what their mother is!"

"I see," said the princess. She thought for a moment, then she stood up and motioned for the tiger and his two charges to follow her. They walked down the sparkling halls of the Emerald Palace until they reached the personal quarters of Princess Ozma.

"Let us see what the Magic Picture has to say," she said, as she pulled the drapes back that cover the large picture on her wall.

"But, how can..." the Hungry Tiger started to ask, but the princess held up a hand for silence.

"Magic Picture," she said, "let me see the mother of the twins, Trixie and Moxie."

The pastoral scene in the huge emerald frame began to swirl and churn and then a new picture began to form. In a dark forest were a man and a woman walking side by side. Their faces were very sad and the woman looked as if she had been crying for a long time.

Both Princess Ozma and the Hungry Tiger looked long and hard at the picture but they could see nothing else.

"I do not understand," said the princess. "The Magic Picture is never wrong; still I do not see the mother of the twins. Perhaps she is hidden in the brush or bushes."

"She must be," agreed the Hungry Tiger.

"Show me Woot, the Wanderer," said the Princess and immediately the picture changed and the Woot Wagon came into focus with the three friends riding merrily along.

"Well, that certainly looks all right," the princess said. "Show me again, the mother of Trixie and Moxie," she requested. Again the picture was turmoil and then it reshaped to show the same man and woman walking in the forest.

"I do not understand," said the Hungry Tiger.

"Nor do I," agreed the princess. "The mother must be hidden right there somewhere! We just can't see her."

"What are we to do?" asked the Hungry Tiger.

"Let us wait until tomorrow and we will ask the picture again," replied Ozma.

CHAPTER NINE:
THE RACING HOGS!

Barney and Two-Bits waited patiently as the shadows grew longer and longer and darkness fell over the Lazy W Ranch. They knew the night was their ally, both in escaping from the muddlumps and in Billy's success in retrieving the golden box.

The young boy had slipped up the rise to the rambling log structure and had taken refuge in the bushes growing around the outside walls. Soon he had worked his way to the window from which the light shone. Carefully he stretched up and peeked over the window sill. Inside the room were the three muddlumps and they were frantically working on the golden box placed on the table before them. One of the men held a pair of pliers, another had a screwdriver and the last held a small hammer. It was quite evident that they had been working on the box for some time as they were quite frustrated with their efforts. As Billy watched, the man with the hammer drew back and smacked the box a hard blow on one side. The boy winced as the hammer struck and he expected to see some type of dent. To his surprise, there was no dent, not even a telltale sign of the blow; however the box seemed to glow brighter than ever as it fairly sparkled and glittered on the table top.

As the Lazy W Ranch hands backed away from the box and conversed in low tones, Billy noticed the box would lose some of it glow. Then when the muddlumps would begin anew in their struggle to force it open, the box would once again glow brightly in the lamplight.

Billy was holding Bouncer up to the window so the little dog could also see what was going on inside the building. "Have you got a plan?" said the dog, turning to the boy.

"Not yet," replied Billy, "but don't worry, I will have before long."

"Have you noticed how they occasionally look toward the door as though they were expecting someone?"

"Yeah," answered the lad. "I think they are looking for their boss, old Bobcat Bob. I think they are afraid of him and don't want him to think they were trying to force the box open. They just can't help but believe it is full of something of value. Boy, if they only knew!"

"I wonder how difficult it would be to get this window open?" the dog asked.

"Let's give it a try," said the boy, grinning at the

prospect.

Carefully the lad situated himself against the wall where he could exert a slow pressure on the frame of the window. Gradually it slid upwards, making only a small amount of noise that went unnoticed by the muddlumps concentrating on the golden box on the table.

"That is enough," said the greyhound when the window had a gap of six inches at the bottom. "If you can slip around to the front of the house and make just enough noise to convince the muddlumps that someone is coming, I can slip into the room and steal the box from under their very noses!"

"What if they see you?" asked Billy, concerned for the safety of the dog. He was rapidly beginning to consider the wire dog as belonging to him.

"Not a problem," the greyhound replied. "They haven't seen me before now, so they won't know where I came from and I'm far too quick for them to catch. I'll have that box and be out this window before they know what happened!"

Billy left the little dog sitting on the window sill watching the activities within the building while he slipped through the shadows to the front of the structure. Once there, he decided to hide himself in a clump of trees growing about twenty meters from the front porch. From his point of concealment, he raised his voice in a high falsetto and shouted loudly.

"Oh, Bobcat Bob! So good to see you again!" Billy was quite pleased with the sound of his voice and the way it carried on the night breeze.

"Yeah?" came a deep reply from just beyond the

trees. "I heard ya but I don't see ya! Where are ya?"

Billy froze in the darkness of the trees. It was Bobcat Bob, just returning as his men had expected. One of the muddlumps appeared in the doorway and waved at the boss of the Rocking W. A large razorback appeared and on his back was the foreman, Bobcat Bob! Billy crouched low and scarcely breathed as the rider moved past his hiding place.

At the first sound of the outside voice, the three muddlumps within the cabin dropped their tools and turned towards the open door. One went to check on Bobcat Bob while the other two busied themselves with activities not involving the golden box while keeping their attention fixed on the front door. They did not notice the small dog leap from the window to floor and then jump onto the table.

Bouncer was very quiet as he nuzzled the box until he could get his jaws in place to hold it. The dog carefully dropped over the edge of the table and bounced up on the window sill. Then he and the golden box were gone.

"Hey, nice work, Billy," grinned the farmer as the boy and dog arrived in the shadows of the barn where their comrades waited.

"Thanks," the boy replied, handing the little dog and box to the farmer mounted on one of the razorbacks. Billy turned and gently stepped into the stirrup of his waiting mount. The animal had a different feel than riding Two-Bits. The hog snorted as the youngster gathered the reins together.

"What are the large bags behind our saddles, Barney?" asked the boy.

The farmer was busy getting the golden box into his bib pocket with one hand and adjusting the wire dog, who didn't want in a pocket, to a position on the front of the saddle with the other one. He didn't immediately answer and it was Two-Bits who spoke up.

"That was my idea, Billy," said the mule. "The bags are full of blue pickles. If that is what keeps these critters calm, then it seems practical that we have a supply."

"Where are we going now?" the boy asked as he nodded in agreement with the assessment of Two-Bits concerning the pickles.

"First and foremost, we want to get away from here," spoke up the farmer who now had the box secure and the dog situated by the pommel of the saddle. "We'll head directly for the trail leading down the side of this mesa. Once on the bottom, we'll decide which way to go."

With Two-Bits leading the way, the trio rode carefully away from the barn on the Lazy W Ranch. Once beyond sight of the buildings, they urged their mounts into a rapid pace and it wasn't long before they were working their way through the darkness of night down the side of the plateau.

They were near the bottom when they heard sounds of pursuit. The noise created by the yelling muddlumps and their mounts was enough to frighten the heartiest of souls.

When Barney and his companions reached the level ground at the bottom of the trail, the path divided in two directions. One, which was over level countryside going to the left, was the road on which they had traveled earlier in the day with the muddlumps. The other trail branched to the right and quickly disappeared into a stand of tall dark trees.

"To the right," called Two-Bits without hesitation and he led the way into the sheltering darkness of the forest. They were just out of sight among the trees when the first of the pursuing muddlumps appeared at the bottom of the plateau. The mule turned off the trail in the trees and presently they came to a small brook where they stopped to rest their mounts and check on the activities of their pursuers.

Quietly they waited and listened. Soon they were convinced Bobcat Bob and his riders had taken the open trail to the left as the sounds of pursuit died away in the darkness.

"I suppose we should keep moving," said Barney with a sigh. "Do you have any idea where we might be headed?"

Two-Bits wagged his head negatively. Then the mule turned to one of the hogs and asked the animal something that neither Barney nor Billy could understand. The two seemed to converse for a short time, then Two-Bits ambled back to Billy and the farmer who were resting beside the trickling stream.

"The hogs say there is another ranch about a two hour ride from here," the mule reported. "It is the O-Bar-Z and we should receive a nice welcome there."

"I must be getting old," complained Barney, "or I'm not used to all this riding. I'm all tuckered out. I'd sure be happy to find a place with a good bed where I could get a good night's sleep."

The mule gave his exasperating bray in lieu of a laugh. "The O-Bar-Z is known for its hospitality. In about two hours or around midnight," the mule added, "you should be making your acquaintance with that bed you wish to meet."

"Let's go," said Barney, getting to his feet.

"May I suggest," said the mule, "that we feed our mounts a few pickles before we start on the trip?"

"Good idea," replied Barney. The farmer and the boy soon had a handful of pickles placed in front of each of the hogs and they were munching happily on the snack.

It was nearing midnight when the two riders, accompanied by the mule, rode up to the front yard of the O-Bar-Z ranch house. The sound of their hoof beats accompanied by the grunting and snorting of the hogs brought an older ranch hand onto the front porch.

"Howdy, gents," the fellow said from the shadows. "Looks like you need a place to bunk for the night."

"Right you are," replied Barney as he stepped down from his razorback. "My friends and I are extremely tired and would certainly appreciate any hospitality you could extend us."

"My name's Rusty," the man said as he shook hands with the farmer and young boy. "I'll call one of the hands to take care of your animals. You come on in and I'll get you a bite to eat before showing you to your bunks."

"I'm Barney and this is Billy," said the tired

rider. "We'll take you up on that bite to eat and a bunk sure sounds good."

Rusty warmed up some stew for the farmer and his companion, then he excused himself to go out and care for the mule and the razorbacks. When he returned, Barney and Billy were just finishing what they both considered to be the best stew they had ever tasted.

"Best we've ever eaten," Barney asserted when Rusty asked how they liked the stew.

The man laughed. "Probably because you've been riding for so long," he said. "Your mule, Two-Bits, said you'd been in the saddle most of the day and near half the night! That's enough to wear anybody out! Come on and I'll show you to your bunks."

Rusty led the way down a long hall that stretched the length of the ranch house. He stopped and opened the door to a small room. Inside were two bunks.

"I'll let you sleep until you wake up," said Rusty, as he turned to leave. "The boss will be back by then."

Barney and Billy both said good night and in less time than it takes to tell it, the two were sound asleep on the bunks. Bouncer curled up beside Barney's pillow with his little muzzle on his outstretched paws and slept as well.

Barney wished that whoever was doing the hammering would stop. He wanted to tell Bertha to go put a stop to the racket but he just couldn't get his eyes open. Then he heard someone shouting and suddenly he sat bolt upright on the bunk.

"Get up you lowdown ornery shysters!" shouted Rusty, his face red from the exertion he had expended in trying to awaken Barney. Billy sat on the opposite bunk, wide eyed and quiet. Bouncer was huddled in his lap.

"What's the matter? What's going on?" Barney asked rubbing the sleep from his eyes.

"You're not gettin' away with it! No siree!" Rusty shouted at the farmer.

Barney shook his head. "What are we trying to get away with?" he asked, rubbing the back of his neck with one hand.

"You're from the Lazy W, that's what!" the man snapped. "You're always trying to sabotage the work here at the O-Bar-Z! I just came from the barn and I saw your saddles! They are both marked with the Lazy W brand!"

"That's simple enough to explain," replied Barney in a calm voice.

"Not to me, you won't!" snapped Rusty. "I'm locking you fellows in the root cellar until the boss gets back! She'll decide what to do with you then!"

"She?" said Barney. "Your boss is a woman?"

Rusty snorted and refused to answer Barney's question. The irate ranch foreman waited while Barney and Billy put on and laced up their shoes. Then he led them out the back door of the ranch house into the morning sunlight and toward the root cellar not far away.

"Get on down there," he said as he held the door for the two visitors. "Don't try to get out 'cause I'm locking the door and if I hear a lot of ruckus down there, it will go hard on you!"

The man and boy were in the dark cellar for what seemed to be a very long time. It was time they put to good use by sleeping.

Rusty returned to the barn and fed the razorbacks and Two-Bits. He was silent as he went about his chores but when he was finished he returned to the stall where Two-Bits was tied.

"I saw the brands on your saddles," he said in an irritated manner. "Reckon you fellows came over from the Lazy W to raise havoc here! I caught you before you got started!"

Two-Bits turned his head toward the foreman. "Lazy W?" questioned the mule. "Not on your life. We escaped those muddlumps last night by slipping away with two of their racing hogs!"

Rusty stood quietly for several moments, reflecting on the words of the mule. "How do I know if you're telling me the truth?" he finally asked.

The mule flopped his ears which is equivalent to one shrugging his shoulders. "Ask the hogs," he said.

Again Rusty thought about the situation. "Well, I would," he said, "but you know as well as I do that hogs aren't very good at talking. Just too blasted lazy, I reckon."

"Want me to talk to them?" Two-Bits asked.

"Well, I suppose you could," replied Rusty, "and I'd just sort of listen. Maybe I could understand enough to know what they say."

Two-Bits raised his head and looked across the walkway toward the razorbacks where they were eating the blue pickles. "Yo, hogs!" he called.

The two pigs were busy slobbering and grunting as they ate. Two-Bits called again and one of the animals raised his head.

"Where did those two guys come from that rode you in here last night?" the mule asked loudly. "Do they work for the Lazy W?"

The two razorbacks continued to chomp and munch on their pickles, not at all concerned with the questions from the mule. One of the hogs continued to hold his head up while he ate and watched the mule.

Two-Bits gathered himself together and then humped his back up and lashed out with his hind legs. His hooves struck the paneling of the stall with a loud crashing sound. Everything in the barn became silent. Even the razorbacks stopped their crunching.

The mule brayed loudly and then carefully repeated his question to the two hogs.

There was a certain amount of 'woofing' and grunting as the pigs conversed with the mule. Rusty stood silently listening, trying to make sense of the conversation.

Finally the hogs went back to eating and the mule turned to the foreman. "Did you understand any of that?" Two-Bits asked.

"Very little," Rusty replied. "I think I did get enough to believe you about not being from the Lazy W. Did I understand that you stole two razorbacks to make your escape from the muddlumps?"

"We just borrowed them," replied the mule. "We figured we'd turn them loose and they'd go back home to get more of those pickles. I don't believe we could have escaped if I had had to carry both Barney and Billy. I was already very tired."

Rusty nodded. "I believe you," he said slowly. "However, I think I'll wait for the boss to get here and let her decide what to do. You reckon your friends will mind too much about staying in the root cellar until then?"

Two-Bits brayed. "My guess is they are both asleep right now. Probably curled up on a pile of carrots or potatoes!"

It was close to noon when the door to the root cellar opened and a shaft of bright sunlight caused both Barney and Billy to sit up and rub their eyes. Two-Bits had been exactly right in that both the man and boy had slept the morning away.

At the top of the stairs stood a tall, dark, curvaceous figure. Then the first form was joined by another one, whom Billy and Barney recognized as the shape of Rusty, the foreman.

"Come on up, boys," he called. "It's time to meet the boss!"

Shielding their eyes from the bright sunlight, Barney and Billy made their way up the cement steps. Bouncer followed at their heels.

"So you are the spies from the Lazy W?" said the young woman facing them. She was tall and lean with dark red hair and a suntanned face that came from spending a considerable amount of time out of doors. She was dressed in jeans, boots, a western style shirt and a wide brimmed Stetson hat. She stood with her hands on her hips and a wide smile on her face.

"Well, not that we were aware of, ma'am," replied Barney, not quite sure what to make of this situation. "We escaped from the Lazy W and it looks like we might have to do the same thing here."

The girl gave a musical laugh. "You'll not need to escape from the O-Bar-Z," she said. "Rusty has filled me in concerning your situation. In fact," she added, "those razorbacks have already eaten all the pickles you brought with you. We don't raise the blue pickles here as they have no value other than to feed hogs, which we don't have. Rusty put the saddles back on the razorbacks and turned them loose to return to the Lazy W about half an hour ago."

Barney nodded. "Does that mean we are free to go?" he asked.

"Sure thing," the girl replied. "However, we'd like to invite you to stay for a while. We are very busy at this time of the year with the steak harvest but we can manage to work in a barbecue this evening. I'll tell the cook and we'll get things cracking!"

"Well," said the farmer, turning to his two companions, "what do you think, fellows? Should we take the young lady up on the invitation?"

Both the boy and the mule nodded agreement and Barney looked back toward the ranch boss.

"My name's Callie," she said, showing a slight bit of embarrassment at having not introduced herself earlier. "Callie Conniption! I run the O-Bar-Z!"

"It's nice to meet you, Miss Conniption," said

the farmer. "I'm Barney and my two friends are Billy and Two-Bits. Mighty good companions to hit the trail with, if I do say so," he added.

Callie Conniption reached out and shook hands with the man and then the boy. Lastly she reached over and rubbed the mule's velvety nose.

"Say, Miss Conniption..." began Barney.

"Call me Callie," the girl broke in, "everybody else does. It doesn't sound right for you to be so formal." She laughed lightly and smiled at the farmer.

"All right, Callie," Barney replied. "I was wondering if there was something we could do to help this afternoon. We are well rested now and I believe you said you were very busy harvesting..." the farmer paused. "Did you say *harvesting* steaks?" he asked.

"Yes," replied the ranch boss with a wide smile on her face. "We grow steaks on earleaf plants. When they are ready for harvest, we go into the fields and pick them for freezing. You have to know just which ones to harvest as some are ready earlier than others. But usually we have the whole crop in storage within a week."

"Earleaf plants?" questioned the farmer. "Never heard of such a crop!"

"They grow like a corn stalk," added Rusty. "The plant gets about four or five feet tall. The leaves look exactly like the ears of cattle! They are even colored black like an Angus or red like a Hereford. I once saw a Holstein plant that had white leaves with black spots. However, the Holstein doesn't produce as good a quality meat and we don't grow the plant here on the ranch."

"I reckon not," agreed the farmer. "The Holstein breed is a milk producing animal, not beef producing."

"The steaks grow very much like an ear of corn," Callie continued. "You have to know just when to pick it and when to leave it on the stalk a while longer. It takes a lot of practice. So, while we'd prefer you not try to help us harvest, you are more than welcome to come to the fields and watch!"

The afternoon proved interesting to Barney, Billy, and Two-Bits as they watched the ranch hands picking the ripe steaks. Even Bouncer had a good time running around and playing in the field.

When they returned to the ranch house that evening, the barbecue was set up in the shade of the trees surrounding the front lawn and all the ranch hands enjoyed the meal with their guests. The sun was below the western horizon and the shadows were growing long when the ranch boss came to the table where Barney and his friends were seated. She laughed lightly and sat down beside the farmer and the boy. Two-Bits, who of course did not eat meat, had settled down in the grass nearby.

"Tell me," said Callie Conniption, "what brings you fellows to the O-Bar-Z?"

"Well," said Barney, pushing his plate back on the table, "I'm just not sure what brought us to this land of yours, other than a flying horse tank, but I do know we are trying to locate a gentleman known as the Prankster. Seems that this fellow has cast a spell over our friend, Two-Bits, and we'd like to get him to reverse it."

Callie pushed her Stetson back, pursed her lips and seemed to be in deep thought. "I believe the Prankster was here on the O-Bar-Z not too long ago. However," and here the young lady paused as though trying to make up her mind on something. "I believe I have the power to help your friend," she finally said.

CHAPTER TEN:
THE MAGIC COWGIRL

"What!" exclaimed Barney. "You can do magic?"

Two-Bits, who had been resting not too far away, had heard the exchange of words and was immediately on his feet and hurrying toward Callie Conniption.

Callie the cowgirl threw her hands up in mock surprise at the sudden interest shown by the mule. Then she reached out and rubbed the top of his head as his ears twitched back and forth in excitement.

"Let us go into the house," she said as she realized just how important this situation was for Two-Bits and his friends. "There are certain things I must do in preparation for this, uh, event!"

"Are you some sort of a witch?" asked Billy as they moved toward the rambling ranch house. "I once heard you had to be some sort of witch to do magic!"

Callie laughed in that light hearted tinkle of hers. "No, Billy," she replied. "I am not a witch and have never had any intention of being one. I like who I am and what I do here on the O-Bar-Z. However, my mother gave me a book of magic many long years ago and I have kept it."

"Have you ever done any of the magic from the book?" asked Barney, beginning to wonder if this was really going to amount to anything.

"Oh, yes," was Callie's reply. "I have done a number of things from the book but since I do not use it very often, I have not committed any of the spells to memory. I must go over the procedure very carefully to make sure I do not make a mistake. The pronunciation must be just perfect or nothing will change when you cast the magic!"

"Oh," replied Barney as they entered the ranch house.

Callie suggested they all wait in the front room by the fireplace while she went upstairs to get the book. Barney and Billy sat down on the couch but Two-Bits was so keyed up that he could not remain still. He wandered about the room being careful not to bump or jar anything since the room was not furnished with the expectations of a mule wandering about the place.

It seemed like a long time before Callie Conniption finally came down the stairs. In her hands she held a rather large book bound in red leather with a blue star imprinted on the cover. She sat down at the table and opened the volume.

"I'm sorry it took me so long to find the book,"

she said. "It has been so long since I have used it that I had forgotten just where I had placed it. It was there, once I looked in the right place," she added as she searched through the pages for the right magical solution.

"Ah, here it is," she said after a few moments. "How to return one to one's former self," she read. "Now," she said, "don't interrupt while I commit this to memory so that I can do it exactly right!"

Everyone was very quiet and even Two-Bits stopped his pacing about the room while Callie studied the magic book. It seemed an eternity to Two-Bits before the girl stood up and silently moved to stand in front of him. She reached out and placed her hands on the top of his head. The mule was trembling all over as the cowgirl began the spell.

Callie's eyes were closed and her lips moved imperceptibly as she began to work the enchantment. Her verbal words were sharp and clear but they were completely unintelligible to Barney and Billy.

For several moments the girl continued chanting with her eyes closed and then the two observers began to notice a change taking place in the mule. He grew smaller in size and his coloring became lighter. A growth began to appear on his head and his tail shortened.

Then Barney and Billy stared speechlessly at the transformation. Before them stood a goat!

The cowgirl stopped her chanting, opened her eyes and stepped back. A smile was on her face.

"It worked!" she said excitedly.

"Oh, boy," said Two-Bits. "Where is a mirror? I've got to see!"

"Right around the corner," said Callie, pointing.

Two-Bits scooted around the corner and then gave a loud bleat of dismay! He was not a reindeer, he was a billy goat!

"What happened?' he cried in anguish. "Did the spell go wrong?"

"What do you mean?" asked Callie. "I changed you back to your former self. Weren't you a billy goat?"

"No, no!" exclaimed Two-Bits. "I was a reindeer, recently retired from the rigors of pulling Santa's sleigh. I came to Oz for a vacation and ran afoul of that no-good fellow known as the Prankster! He changed me into a mule and banished me from the magical kingdom. I am back and with the help of my friends, I am searching for that foul creature that did this to me!"

"I am sorry," apologized the cowgirl. "That was the right magical enchantment. It should have worked." She went immediately to her big book and began looking over the instructions for invoking the reversal of the magic spell.

Barney came and looked over her shoulder. Then Billy peered over the opposite shoulder but the book was all written words and he could not read. He moved away, filled with the deep urge to learn to read and write.

"I did it correctly," she finally said. "Would you like me to try it again? I would have to wait for twenty-four hours but we could give it another shot if you'd like?"

"Let me think about it," Two-Bits replied. "I'm no worse off now than I was before. I'm a little smaller but my head sure feels better with something on it!" He was referring to the horns of the goat replacing the antlers of the reindeer.

"Pardon me," said Barney from where he stood still looking at the magic book on the table. "I think it looks like someone has changed some of the things written in this book, Callie."

A surprised look crossed the girl's face and she returned immediately to the table. The Kansas farmer pointed to a spot that looked a little smudged.

"I think some of the words of the incantation have been changed. See right here, and again over here? Not much and done very carefully," the man said. "Whoever was responsible for the changes seemed to know what they were doing. I don't believe they were trying to ruin the spell, just make it different."

Callie was looking at the book intently. "Yes," she said, "I see it now. I was so intent on getting the spell just right that I didn't notice those imperceptible changes!"

"Golly, I wonder who would do something like that?" said Billy.

Barney looked at Callie and asked, "Did you say the Prankster was here on the ranch not too long ago?"

"About a month or so back," the girl replied. "Rusty made the comment when the Prankster left that we were lucky he hadn't pulled any mischievous tricks during his stay. Now it looks as though he did!"

Barney nodded. "I believe he did," he replied.

"I believe," said Two-Bits, now a goat, "that we must find the Prankster in order for me to return to my normal self."

"How do you plan to get him to change you back?" asked Callie. "I believe he is a very self-centered individual and will only do what he wants to do. You'll have to think of a way to get him to want to turn you back into your reindeer form!"

"We'll cross that bridge when we get to it," replied Barney, nodding his head slowly. "I've been giving that persuasion thing a lot of thought but haven't come up with a plan as yet!" Then he turned and looked at Two-Bits. "We will, though!" he declared.

"Which way do we go now?" asked Billy with a laugh. "I thought I did a lot of traveling with my former two companions but that was nothing compared to going with you two guys."

"According to what the Prankster said," replied Callie, "he was going to go over to the Candy Caverns. They really aren't far from here. You can walk it in a day."

"Good," said Two-Bits. "Just give us some instructions on how to get there."

"Sure, I'll be glad to do that," replied the cowgirl. "However, I'd like to go with you! I want that Prankster to straighten out my book of magic. I've got a little magic of my own and I might make it rough on him! Now, with a second thought, I'm not all that certain we'll find him at the Candy Caverns! He never stays anywhere very long as he usually wears out his welcome!"

"We'd sure like to have you accompany us," replied the farmer. "Can you be ready at first light tomorrow?"

"Oh!" exclaimed Callie. "I can't go just yet! I've got to see to it all the steaks are harvested and frozen properly. That will take a few days yet."

"We'll get to those caverns as quickly as we can," replied Barney. "You finish up here and then join us in our search for the Prankster. Surely we are getting closer."

Callie Conniption agreed with the planning of her visitors. Soon Barney and Billy were headed for their bunks and Two-Bits was on his way to the stable. They planned an early start the following morning for the Candy Caverns.

CHAPTER ELEVEN: THE BURLEY BEAR

Woot, the Wanderer, the Shaggy Man, and the Tin Woodman rolled along on the Woot Wagon traveling deeper and deeper into the dark recesses and unexplored back lands of the Gillikin Country. They traveled around mountains, crossed plains and rivers, and skirted those areas where the Woot Wagon could not travel. Always they were working their way to the northeast as that is where it was thought they would find Captain Fyter.

"We seldom see a soul out here," Woot said as they rolled up the side of a hill. "You would wonder if Captain Fyter would waste his time in a vacant area like this."

"His job is to keep the peace among the wild peoples of the north lands," said the Shaggy Man. "He travels by foot so he would not have quick access in and out of any particular place. I believe we shall find him by and by."

"Pardon me," said the Tin Woodman, "but do my eyes see a cabin far up the side of that hill? Somewhere in the shadows by those tall pines."

Both the Shaggy Man and Woot shaded their eyes as they peered toward the spot where Nick Chopper indicated.

"I believe there is," said Woot. "Shall we take a run up there and check it out?"

"I think we should," said the Shaggy Man. "We must check every possibility in our effort to locate our friend."

Woot turned the vehicle and they began their ascent of the rather steep hill. Before long they could see the structure that the Tin Woodman had spotted earlier.

"It certainly doesn't look to have been used for a while," commented the Shaggy Man as they came to a stop by the building. "Let's give it a quick look-see and be on our way."

The three friends stepped off the Woot Wagon and began looking over the cabin. The building had been made of wood and then covered with some type of plaster coating on the outside. Obviously it had sported a coat of paint at one time, but that had mostly weathered away with age. The windows were covered with dust and cobwebs.

"Door won't budge," said the Shaggy Man as he stepped away from the entrance. "It has most likely been closed up too long."

The Tin Woodman had gone around to the back side of the building and Woot was standing at one corner looking outward.

"You can see where someone once had a garden," the boy said, pointing toward a cleared area that was now covered with grass and weeds.

"Hey, fellows," called the Tin Woodman from the rear of the house. "I found an opening."

Woot and the Shaggy Man hurried to the back side of the building. The Tin Woodman was nowhere in sight but there was a large hole dug into the wall. Then a growling sound came from the interior.

"Tin Woodman," called Woot, "are you all right?" More growling came from the hole and then the back side of Nick Chopper came pushing outwards.

"My pardon, madam," he was saying as he exited. "I thought the building was empty!"

Following him from the hole was a large burley bear. She did not seem particularly upset as she immediately shook her coat and the dust flew in all directions.

"Now that is something I cannot do," commented Nick who had retreated to the vicinity of his friends.

The bear stopped shaking and looked at him. "Well," she said, "as anyone can plainly see, you wear your skin too tight!"

"We are quite sorry to have disturbed you," the Tin Woodman apologized again. "We are looking for a friend who may be in need of our help. We thought he might be here."

"Would that he were," growled the burley bear. "Then I could have my cave back!"

"Do you know where to find our friend?" asked Woot. "We believe he had need of our help."

"That I do," the bear replied. "He is in my cave and he seems to have no inclination to leave. I believe he may be injured."

"And just where would we find this cave?" asked the Shaggy Man.

"Normally I don't go around giving out the location of my cave," the bear growled, "but for you, my shaggy one," and her eyes glowed warmly, "I will tell you."

The burley bear grunted a bit and then she sat down and leaned back against the cabin wall. "Go that way," she said and pointed with her nose, "until you reach what is left of an old road. Follow it to the edge of a canyon on your left. Stand at the edge and look up the canyon. You will see a small cave. There you will find your friend. Good luck."

With that, the burley bear got to her feet and began wriggling herself back into the old deserted cabin.

The three companions looked at each other and then quietly hurried around to the front of the dilapidated shack, got on the Woot Wagon and moved in the direction indicated by the bear.

They thought perhaps they had missed the road when at last they discovered it. They followed the path as directed by the bear and it wasn't too long before they came to the edge of the canyon. Sure enough, as they stood on the upper rim and looked down, they could see a small cave.

"Let's not waste time," said Woot. "Let us see if Captain Fyter lies bound within the cave below us."

With that, all three began working their way down the steep slope toward the bottom and the cave.

It was not an easy descent, but they finally reached the bottom and began walking toward the cave. As they approached, they would hear light groans coming from within the dark opening.

The Tin Woodman stopped. "This is not right," he said. "I do not believe Captain Fyter would be groaning."

They advanced slowly and cautiously. In a few moments they could see the bottoms of a pair of boots protruding from the cave opening. Soon they were beside the lean dark form of a man suffering from fever and dehydration. He seemed to be somewhat delirious. Further examination revealed his left leg was broken both above and below the knee.

"First," said the Shaggy Man, "we must set those bones. Then we must find flat pieces of wood and splint them. Finally, we must get him out of here and find water if he is to survive."

Woot forced a small amount of water between the parched lips of the suffering man while the Shaggy Man and the Tin Man set the bones in the leg. Then Nick Chopper used his axe and they soon had some nice flat boards to use as splints. Woot went to his wagon and retrieved a coil of cord he carried in the storage space beneath the second seat. Soon the splints were bound in place.

"Getting him up that slope is going to be a problem," commented the Tin Man. "I think I could carry him but I could stumble or fall and that would not be good for this fellow."

"I suggest we fix a drag so that we can pull him slowly up the canyon wall," said the Shaggy Man. "Two long poles and that big coat of his should do the trick."

A few moments later they had fashioned two poles. They carefully lifted the injured man to remove the coat and discovered a large book lying under his coat that they had not noticed earlier. The title read, *The Prankster's Book of Phine Pranks*.

They removed the coat and fastened it across the poles. Then they lifted the injured man again and placed him on the drag. The Tin Man took the ropes tied to the front of the drag and commenced working his way up the slope, pulling the injured man behind him.

The Shaggy Man and Woot returned to the cave to pick up any remaining items belonging to the unconscious man. The old man picked up the book and flipped through it for a short time.

"This looks like a book of magic to me," he said to Woot. "Princess Ozma has decreed that magic should not be practiced in Oz anymore. I'm thinking this book should be turned over to her." The boy nodded in agreement.

It took a long while, but they finally reached the top of the slope with the unconscious man.

"Now, we need water and lots of it," said the Shaggy Man. "I suggest we go forward in our search. We know it would be a long way back to any sizable amount of water."

CHAPTER TWELVE: TURMOIL IN THE CAVERNS

The next morning Barney, Billy, and Two-Bits bid goodbye to Callie Conniption, the boss of the O-Bar-Z, and were well on the road toward the Candy Caverns before the sun rose above the horizon. Knowing they were good travelers, they expected to reach the fabled candy tunnels much sooner than estimated by Callie, who planned to join them in two or three days' time.

By noon they were off the O-Bar-Z range and moving in a southeasterly direction when they detected a large cloud of dust coming their way.

"I'm going to suggest," said Barney as he observed the approaching cloud, "that we take cover until we determine what is raising that dust."

Two-Bits and Billy agreed and they quickly hid themselves in the brush growing a short distance up the slope from the road.

It soon became obvious to Barney and his companions that it was a group of riders mounted on strange looking animals. As the riders came closer, they were recognized as a group of muddlumps riding creatures that appeared to be some form of a large lizard. The mounts were a light green in color with black stripes, resembling those of a zebra, crossing their bodies. Their long black tongues kept flicking in and out as they moved. Their running motion, being that of a lizard, was what was stirring up the dust in the road.

"I think," said Two-Bits, "that I shall wander down to the road and see what I can learn. They may be looking for a man and a boy and a mule, but certainly they are not looking for a goat!" He bleated softly and ambled on down the hillside to the road. He arrived at the same time as the mounted muddlumps. Their leader raised his long thin arm and the troop reined their mounts to a stop.

The lead muddlump stared hard from his saddle at the lone goat chewing his cud by the roadside.

"I say, goat," he called out in his hissing manner of speaking, "have you seen any strangers in these parts?"

"No, can't say as I have," the goat replied as Barney and Billy certainly were not strangers to him. "Just what sort of stranger are you looking for?" he asked.

"A man, a boy and a mule!" the leader replied. "They stole a couple of fast razorbacks from the Lazy W," he added.

"Well, they shouldn't be hard to spot with a

couple of riding hogs," answered the goat.

"Oh, the razorbacks got away and came home," said the muddlump. "Those fellows are out here somewhere on foot and old Bobcat Bob is rather anxious to get his hands on them! If you see them, get word to old Bobcat!"

The goat nodded and continued to chew.

With that the muddlump leader gave an overhead signal and the mounted search party rode down the road. Two-Bits watched them go until they were out of sight.

Presently Barney and Billy joined Two-Bits by the roadside. They had been close enough to hear the entire conversation.

"I reckon we'll have to be real careful from here on to the Candy Caverns," said Barney.

"Uh-huh," agreed Two-Bits. "I'm thinking we'd better check out the situation at the caverns before we just go marching in. They might be friends of those Lazy W fellows, too."

"We'd better keep a close watch both fore and aft," Barney muttered, "and we might as well get to hoofing it!" With that the three friends started again for the Candy Caverns.

It was late afternoon when they arrived at a rocky ridge that had a small castle set deeply into the side of the slope. The structure was made of stone but had been painted to resemble colorful candy pieces.

"Will you look at that!" Billy exclaimed as they came in sight of the fabled caverns.

"Looks like the whole thing is made out of giant pieces of taffy," said Barney.

"Might I suggest," said the goat, "the two of you stay out of sight until I check out what sort of reception is in store for us."

"Sure thing, Two-Bits," replied the farmer. "Billy and I shall wait for your return." With that the man and boy sought concealment not far from the candy colored walls of the castle. They lay down in the shade of some large leafy bushes and stretched out on the grassy turf where they could watch Two-Bits. They were quite tired from the day's walk and wanted to take advantage of any rest time they could get.

Bouncer hopped out of Barney's pocket, where he had spent the day riding and snoozing, and began playing in the grass.

The goat ambled down the road as nonchalant and carefree as he could manage. An attendant appeared as Two-Bits approached the gate.

"Good evening, sir," said the goat. "I trust all is well in the Candy Caverns?"

"Indeed, my friend," the fellow replied.

"Tell me," said the goat, "have you been visited by a group of riders from the Lazy W Ranch?"

"That we have," said the attendant, his eyes narrowing as though he did not like the thought. "Fortunately, Farf came along about that same time and sent them on their way!"

"Ah, I see," said Two-Bits, "and just who is Farf?"

"Oh, that's Far Flung, one of our candy scientists," replied the gate keeper, "but everybody just calls him Farf. He and his twin brother, Nurf, do all the mental work in the Candy Caverns."

"Nurf?" questioned Two-Bits.

"Oh, yes," the gate man said. "That's short for Near Enough."

"So Farf and Nurf have no liking for the muddlumps from the Lazy W?" said Two-Bits. He turned toward the brush where Barney and Billy were watching the proceedings and bobbled his head. That was their signal and the two scrambled to their feet and approached the castle gate where they joined Two-Bits.

"Would it be possible to visit with whoever is in charge of the Candy Caverns?" asked Barney.

"That would be Farf and Nurf," the gate man said in a very agreeable tone. "Follow me." He led the three travelers into the castle where they crossed an ornately decorated hallway that stretched from right to left. They approached two bright red doors trimmed in a chocolate brown color. The gate man swung the doors open wide and bowed to the visitors.

"You may enter the candy caverns," he said in a very formal voice. "Continue down the tunnel and you will come to several rooms where candy is being made. Pass through the caramel workrooms and you will see a bright lemon colored door. There you will find Farf and Nurf."

The tunnel ahead of them was a bright red in color and curved sharply to their right. They thanked the gate man and began following the winding tunnel. They had not gone far when they came upon two workmen using roller brushes with long handles to paint the tunnel walls. They stopped for a moment to watch. One painter was putting on a coat of red, while his fellow worker was adding a diagonal white stripe.

"You know," said Billy, "that sure looks like peppermint candy they are painting on that wall." He quickly stepped forward and dabbed his finger into the red paint and stuck it in his mouth, much to the dismay of Barney.

"Yep," replied the boy, "that's what it is! They are painting the walls with candy!"

"Yes," said one of the painters, as he stopped to dip his roller in a bucket of soft peppermint. "This is the favorite flavor of Farf and Nurf. If you like, there is a tasting pole not far down the tunnel. Feel free to taste all you want."

Barney thanked the two workers and they continued down the tunnel which was dropping lower underground as they walked along. Soon they came to the tasting pole which looked like nothing more than a barber pole sitting in the middle of the floor. The base of the pole contained a small sign that said, *Tasting Pole - Select Flavor* and there were numerous buttons to punch. Barney read the sign aloud and Billy quickly selected a flavor and punched the button. Immediately the top of the pole flopped open forming a small table containing a dish filled with the chosen flavor.

"Wow, this is neat!" exclaimed Billy.

Bouncer hopped down from Barney's pocket and selected a butter cream. He pushed the button with his nose and soon had his choice.

Barney chose a flavor and then Two-Bits picked one. Soon all three adventurers and the wire dog were munching on their favorite flavors of candy as they continued down the candy coated tunnel.

Presently the floor leveled out and they came to a wide open area. Here there were many tables with a great number of candy makers busy with their duties of making candy. Barney, Billy and Two-Bits began to walk through the caramel work area toward the opposite side where they could see the bright lemon colored doors.

"Look over to your left," whispered Barney. "There are two monkeys just working away like they knew what they were doing! Sort of gives new meaning to the phrase, 'untouched by human hands,' doesn't it?"

Several of the workers waved or nodded as the visitors wound their way through the big candy making kitchen. Both of the monkeys waved right along with their fellow workers.

"They sure do look sad," commented Billy. "The monkeys, I mean. Surely they aren't held here against their will."

Barney knocked on the bright yellow doors and a deep voice from within bade them enter. The farmer opened the door and they stepped into what was obviously a laboratory. Two men in long frock coats were working at various projects.

"Good afternoon," said the first man, "welcome to the Candy Caverns! That is, if you came for a visit and not with some ulterior motive up your sleeve!"

"Hi," said the second man, turning to see who his brother had spoken to. He grinned at them and Barney noticed immediately that the two men were exactly alike. Twins, no doubt.

"What Farf means is that recently we had a visitor who was up to no good. While we certainly welcome visitors, we absolutely do not need the trouble of a joker or a self-styled humorist!"

"I am Barney Fields," said the farmer reaching out to shake hands with the two men. "This is Billy and Two-Bits. We have been following a fellow known as the Prankster and thought he might have been here."

The two brothers looked at each other and nodded. "He was here," said Farf. "We couldn't put up with his antics."

"So, we just used the Illuminator Transporter on him," chimed in Nurf. "Enough was enough!"

"Just what did he do?" asked Two-Bits.

"First," said Farf, "he caused several of our flavors to take on non-candy tastes. Our lemon began to taste like dill pickles. Our raspberry tasted like burned popcorn! However, when he changed two of our workers into monkeys, that was it!"

"Zappo!" exclaimed Nurf. "We got him out of here!"

"We have been following him for a good while now," explained Barney. "He put his hex on our friend, Two-Bits. We want him to reverse the spell."

"He told us the spell was irreversible," said Farf, a perplexed look on his face.

"I don't believe that is true," said Barney and he proceeded to tell the two brothers of their experience with Callie the Cowgirl.

"We really believe Callie could have reversed the spell if the Prankster hadn't messed up her magic book," he finished. "That would indicate to us that there is hope, but first we must find that fellow!"

"What are you going to do to get him to reverse his spell? He was adamant that it could not be changed when he was here."

"We don't know," said Barney, rubbing his head as though in thought. "We'll come up with something. We've got to get him in a situation where he needs our help, then maybe he'll be willing to negotiate."

Nurf went to the door and spoke to someone outside and in moments the two monkeys appeared.

"I'd like you to meet Burt and Art," said Farf. "They've been with us since we first started the factory. That was way, way back. You can see what the Prankster did to them."

Barney shook hands with the two monkeys, knowing they were really men who had been changed by magic, like Two-Bits.

Farf explained to the two monkeys about Barney and his friends trying to follow the Prankster in an effort to get the spell reversed.

"We'd like to go with you," said Burt and Art nodded his head vigorously.

"If there is any chance we can be returned to our former self, we'll take it," Art added.

"You are more than welcome to accompany us," replied Barney.   Bouncer went over to check out the two monkeys and decided he liked them as they scratched his chin and rubbed his ears. They acted like human beings but they looked like monkeys.

"We need to know where the Prankster was going when he left here," the farmer said, looking at Farf and Nurf. "You said something about causing him to leave. Do you have any idea where he was going?"

"Well, yes and no," replied Farf. "Come. We will show you the Illuminator Transporter."

Barney and his friends followed the two candy scientists into an adjoining room. He had trouble deciding if the place looked like a mad scientist's laboratory or like a kitchen for cooking candy. There were large kettles all about the room along with tubes that seemed to be running everywhere. All the items were made of a clear material. Some of the tubes were very large and some were quite tiny with varying sizes in between.

"Here," said Farf, "is the Illuminator Transporter. We just put something inside this large tube, close the door, set the dial and send the occupant where ever it is we want him to go!"

"We just caught the Prankster," said Nurf, "and tossed him in there. Then slammed the door and pulled the lever. He went to a wild part of the Gillikin Country where he can't do us any more harm!"

"So this contraption will transport you anywhere you want to go?" asked Barney. "Would it send us to the same place as you sent the Prankster?"

"Indeed it would," said Nurf.

"How long before we can be after the Prankster," asked Two-Bits.

"It takes it about half an hour to get revved up and ready to transport," said Farf. "I'll turn it on now and in a little while you can be on your way!"

"I understand the 'transporter' part of your name," said Barney, "but where does the 'illuminator' part come in?"

"Oh," said Farf, "when one is ready to transport, he becomes very much transparent and something like gelatin in texture. The person also has an aura or a shine about him. When you arrive at your destination you will be suspended in the air until your body regains its shape and weight. As this happens, you will gradually descend until by the time you are back to normal you'll be standing on the ground."

"It's all quite simple and harmless," added Nurf when he saw the perplexed look on Barney's face.

"Why was such a machine invented?" asked Barney.

"It's a much easier way to send workers to exotic places to gather the many flavors we need in our candy making. Our people love to travel by way of the Illuminator Transporter," answered Farf.

"Say," said the farmer, "a while ago I mentioned Callie Conniption from the O-Bar-Z Ranch."

"Oh, yes," the brothers replied, almost in unison. "Callie is one of our best customers," said Farf.

"She is definitely one of the prettiest," added Nurf.

"When Callie is finished with the steak harvest on the ranch," said Barney, "she is going to come here to find out where we went in our search for the Prankster. Can you send her after us in the Illuminator Transporter?"

"We sure can," answered Farf.

"While we are waiting for the machine to warm up," said Nurf, "why don't we all go down to the cafeteria and get a bite to eat before you take off?"

Farf and Nurf, Barney and his companions, and the two monkeys were soon on their way to the lunch room.

CHAPTER THIRTEEN: THE GUARDIAN OF THE WATERFALL

The occupants of the Woot Wagon rolled along at a good rate of speed for some time. The trace of the road they were following was winding farther and farther back in the mountains with more twists and turns the deeper they went.

"I don't understand this," said the Shaggy Man. "We certainly should have found water before now. The forest and vegetation, it all suggests water! Yet we have found none. This poor fellow is in dire need of water!"

"We have a little left in our canteens," said Woot. "We can use that for tonight and perhaps we will have better luck tomorrow."

The sun had dropped below the horizon and darkness was falling. In the shadows of the mountains, it was becoming difficult to see clearly for any distance ahead of them. Woot had slowed his wagon to a very slow speed.

"Yes, I think perhaps we should stop for the night," the Shaggy Man agreed.

Shortly, they found a place beside the trail and Woot moved the wagon into the shelter of the trees. They started a small fire for warmth and used what water they had left to alleviate the suffering of the injured man. Woot and the Shaggy Man were both tired from the long day and were stretched out by the fire resting. The Tin Woodman, who does not get tired because he is not made of meat and bones, decided to take a walk in the dark trees surrounding their camp.

"I shall return in a short while," he told his companions as he waved and turned into the dark shadows of the forest. His ever present axe was in his right hand.

The Tin Woodman had been gone only a short time when Woot suddenly raised his head and listened intently.

"Do you hear anything?" he asked, turning to the Shaggy Man.

The older fellow opened his eyes and rose up on an elbow, listening. Beside him lay the book he had picked up in the small cave. He had attempted to look at it but the firelight was not bright enough for him to make out the inscriptions.

"Yes," he said, "I hear it now. It sounds like someone singing! What do you suppose it could mean?"

Both Woot and the Shaggy Man were on their

feet when the shadows appeared at the edge of the small clearing. Suddenly the singing stopped and the shadows became nothing more than just shadows.

"Come join us by our fire," the Shaggy Man finally called out in moderate tones. "We are travelers and will cause you no harm."

There was silence and a barely discernible movement in the shadows.

"We are caring for an injured man and we are in urgent need of water," the old man continued when his first effort brought no response.

"Could you tell us where to find water?" Woot called softly.

The shadows moved slightly and the boy and old man found themselves facing two young girls with drawn bow and arrows. One arrow was pointed at each of them as the girls advanced carefully.

Woot knelt slowly near the fire and held out his hands for warmth. "Come," he said, "warm yourselves by the fire." While the night air was cool, it was not yet cold.

The pair moved cautiously forward. They were dressed in fringed leather garments and their long hair was pulled together at the back with a leather piece and hung down their backs. Their footwear resembled moccasins more than the elfin slippers often preferred by the inhabitants of Oz. The two girls were about the same height and looked enough alike to be sisters.

One of the visitors made a soft noise and nodded toward the form of the ill man lying by the side of the Woot Wagon. The other one glanced quickly and then nodded. They both lowered their weapons although they still held them ready for use.

"We see you speak the truth," said the girl nearer the fire.

"Yes," replied the Shaggy Man. "We found this poor fellow in a cave some distance from here. He suffers a broken leg and is very weak and in desperate need of water."

"Our gourds are empty," said the second girl, referring to the water gourds hanging from the belts at their waists. "The day has been long, but we shall soon be home," she added as an explanation for the empty gourds.

"If we just knew where to find water," said Woot, "we would go there yet tonight. The fellow is in dire need of water."

The two girls looked at each other and nodded in mutual agreement. "I am Mara," said the first one, who seemed to be the leader and was probably the older of the two. "This is Clara, my sister. We can tell you how to get to water just a short distance from here. You will have to leave the trail to reach it."

"Thank you," said the Shaggy Man, "and just how do we find this water?"

For the next few moments the girls gave explicit directions for finding the water hole. It was a ways up the trail they were following and then off to one side and just over a rise. A spring had created a small pool and it was excellent drinking water according to the girls.

"Our father will be out looking for us soon if we don't show up at home," Mara said, "so we must go now." They moved over to the still form on the ground for a look at the injured man before leaving.

As the four of them stood looking at the sunken cheeks and drawn face of the fevered man, his eyelids fluttered momentarily. Then his dry lips moved and it sounded as if he were asking for water. The two girls backed away while Woot and the Shaggy Man knelt by their patient.

While the two fellows were intent on hearing the words of the ill man, Clara went to the log where the Shaggy Man had been resting and picked up the book that lay in the shadow and slipped it inside her leather jerkin. The two girls stepped quickly to the edge of the clearing, where they said a hurried goodbye and disappeared into the forest.

"Well, I guess that was all he was going to say," said the Shaggy Man, rising to his feet. "Let's get him loaded onto the wagon so that we can leave as soon as the Tin Woodman returns."

Woot and the Shaggy Man lifted the wrapped form of the unconscious man and placed him on the vehicle. They had just finished straightening his covering when Nick Chopper walked into the clearing carrying an armload of wood for the night's campfire.

"Good news," called Woot. "We just had two visitors who told us where to find water and we have our friend already loaded. Let's extinguish the campfire and be on our way."

Shortly, having tidied up the camp area and seeing nothing left, they mounted the Woot Wagon and started up the path. Soon they came to the first landmark, a large rock. Then they came to a broken tree. Here the Shaggy Man got off the wagon and walked. Woot followed slowly in the vehicle while counting the old man's steps. When they had reached one hundred, they stopped.

"Say, listen," said Woot, whose ears were good at catching sounds. "I think I hear water. Do you hear it?"

Both the Shaggy Man and the Tin Woodman agreed.

"I believe they said it was to the left," said the Shaggy Man, "but this seems to be coming from the right."

"Yes, that is so," agreed Woot. "Perhaps they were coming down the trail instead of going up. That would put it on their left."

With that explanation being satisfactory, they turned off the trail and moved toward the sound of splashing water. Presently, in the dark of the trees, they came to a low stone wall about two feet in height.

The moon was just rising above the tree tops and they could see a tall dark cliff rising a short distance beyond the wall. Gushing from a hole nearly a hundred feet high on the side of the stone slab was a large stream of clear water. The water bounced and splashed its way down the cliff. It swirled and churned at the bottom where it formed a pool, then it ran a short distance and dropped through a large hole where if disappeared from sight. The total distance for the water above the ground surface was less than two hundred paces and that included the one hundred foot drop.

For a moment Woot, the Shaggy Man and the

Tin Man stood gazing at the beautiful moonlit sight. Then they heard a noise from the Woot Wagon and they all hurried to see if the injured man was regaining consciousness.

The man's eyes were open and he was calling in a barely audible whisper for water. They picked him up carefully, crossed the low stone wall and placed him gently by the gurgling water. The man's eyes looked clear in the moonlight.

"What is your name, my friend?" asked the Shaggy Man.

"Tommy," came the hoarse whisper. "Please, water!"

Woot dipped his empty canteen into the water and then gently held it to the man's mouth. The fellow's dry throat worked spasmodically as he swallowed the life giving water. Then he lay back quietly.

"Shouldn't give the water to him too fast," the Shaggy Man suggested.

The man groaned, calling again for water. Woot held the canteen so that it trickled gently down the man's parched throat. Presently a pleased relaxed look came over the fellow's face and he dropped into a light sleep.

"He certainly looks better with a little water in him," said the Shaggy Man. "I think I'll get my canteen and fill it. That water sure looks good."

The old man had just turned away from the waters when a shout startled all of them except the sleeping man.

"Halt!" came the cry. Coming toward them was an elderly man running quickly and holding his hand in the air as though to stay whatever was happening. "Do not drink the water!" he shouted as he neared them.

"Why?" asked Woot, thinking that water should be free where ever it was.

"These are the Forbidden Waters," he panted as he came to a stop before them. "You must not drink here!"

"Why not?" asked the Shaggy man, becoming just a little irritated with the stranger who was telling thirsty people they could not drink his water. "Just who are you to make such demands?"

"I am the Guardian of the Forbidden Water," he said. "That is my official title and it is my responsibility to see that no one drinks this water. This is the Forbidden Water. It surfaces only here and in the great Emerald City of Oz. It is the water of forgetfulness. I am so glad I got here in time to stop any of you from taking a drink." He sat down on the low stone fence and wiped his hand across his face as he panted to catch his breath.

Woot, the Shaggy Man, and the Tin Woodman had all taken an involuntary step backwards when the Guardian had mentioned the water for Princess Ozma's Forbidden Fountain. They were well aware of the consequences when one drank that water.

"How much, do you suppose," asked Woot slowly, "one would have to drink for it to take affect? Like, perhaps a glass full?"

"Oh, no," said the Guardian, shaking his head. "One drop will do it. One drop and you will forget everything you ever knew! Absolutely everything!"

Woot turned to one side and emptied his canteen

on the ground.

"Let it dry until there is no moisture inside before you fill it with good water," the Guardian said. Then the man realized the three visitors were all looking at a figure on the ground. He gave a gasp and pointed.

"Did he drink the water?" he asked.

"Yes," replied the Tin Man. "My companions and I found him some distance from here with a broken leg and a bad fever. We have set the leg and were searching for water to alleviate the temperature."

"We gave him water from this pool," the Shaggy Man finished. "We did not know."

The boy knelt beside the sleeping man and gently shook his shoulder. "Tommy," he said. "Wake up." Then he carefully shook the shoulder again.

The man's eyes opened and he looked straight at Woot. "Why are you shaking my shoulder and why did you call me Tommy?"

"If your name is not Tommy," said Woot, "then what is it?"

The man thought for a moment and then replied. "I do not know what my name is? Where are we? Who are we? What are your names?"

The three adventurers looked at the Guardian who was shaking his head hopelessly.

"How did you happen to come to the falls through the forest? Most folks use the road right over there," and he pointed. "Of course, no one wants a drink, they just want to look."

"We were camped not too far down the road,"

said the Shaggy Man. "Then two young girls came into our camp and told us about the water up here. They were in a hurry to get home and did not stay, but they gave us good instructions except they said the water is on the other side of the road."

"Oh, it is," agreed the Guardian. "The good water, that is. Now you say two young girls were in your camp? Did they tell you their names?"

"Oh, yes," replied Woot. "They were Mara and Clara."

"I thought so," replied the Guardian. "Were you missing anything after they left? They are not very trustworthy and have been known to steal things."

"We don't have much," replied Woot, "so there wasn't much they could take."

The Tin Woodman was looking again at the injured man who was sleeping so peacefully. "What are we to do with this fellow?" he asked. "I doubt that he will be in much shape to continue with us in our search."

"Ah," said the Guardian. "Just leave him with us. I have three helpers up at the house and they spend their time in training people who accidentally drank the water, and I don't mind saying, they always turn out to be better people than they previously were. My helpers teach them all good things and they have no memory of their bad side, whatever it might have been. However, it does take a while," he added with a soft laugh.

The Tin Woodman gently picked up the sleeping Tommy and followed the Guardian as he led the way back to his house which was just beyond the trees and not far from the steep cliff.

"I believe you fellows said something about searching," the Guardian said. "Care to tell me what you are looking for? I might be able to help."

"Do you know a Tin Soldier by the name of Captain Fyter?" the Shaggy Man asked.

"Oh, sure," the fellow replied. "Captain Fyter comes by every so often and we spend an afternoon just visiting. The Captain has been to so many interesting places."

"So, do you know where he is now?" asked the Tin Woodman as they approached the house where they would find aid for Tommy.

"No, can't say that I know where he is, although it is about time for him to drop by again."

"From what direction does he usually come when he visits you?" asked the Shaggy Man as they entered the house.

The Guardian cautioned them to be very quiet as his helpers were all sleeping and he would not want to awaken them. They found a bunk and placed the sleeping Tommy in it and then returned to the outdoors.

"Well," said the man, once they were outside again, "I can't really say because I don't usually see him approaching, but when I have, he has come from either direction about the same number of times."

"Then I would think we would continue in the same direction we have been going," said the Tin Woodman. "We believe he is not behind us."

"Yes," agreed the Guardian, "just continue on the road around the corner and through the mountains. In about a day's walk you can be near the plains again."

The man had continued to refer to the faint forest trail as a road, but the travelers did not say anything as one man's trail is another man's road, as it were.

"We shall camp by the good water and be on our way early in the morning," said the Shaggy Man. "We certainly thank you for the information you have given us."

The travelers waved as they returned to the Woot Wagon and the Guardian returned to his house.

CHAPTER FOURTEEN: TRAVELING THE ILLUMINATOR TRANSPORTER

Barney Fields was just a little bit apprehensive about stepping into the machine that looked more like it should be making candy syrup than sending people to far off places. The machine was not large enough to transport everyone at the same time. Billy and Two-Bits had volunteered to go first.

The farmer watched as the interior of the Illuminator Transporter became cloudy and the figures of his friends became very indistinct. Gradually he realized he could no longer see them. They had been transported.

Barney took a deep breath and stepped into the machine. In his pocket was bouncer, the little baling wire dog. The two monkeys hopped in beside him. The door was closed and it was beginning to get foggy around them. That was all he remembered until he realized he was slowly descending.

He opened his eyes and saw Billy and Two-Bits standing a few feet away watching him slowly drift downward. Then his feet were on the ground and the two monkeys were beside him.

"Say, that was pretty neat!" exclaimed Billy. "I could get used to traveling like that." Barney still wasn't too sure. Bouncer scrambled out of his pocket and jumped to the ground, glad to be outside again.

The monkeys assured the farmer and his companions they were, indeed, in the Gillikin Country. They were standing near a crossroads but they had no way of knowing just which direction the Prankster might have gone.

"I suspect we need to go until we find someone who may have seen our man," said Two-Bits. "I definitely feel like we are getting closer to him."

"In that case," said Barney, "have you got a feeling as to which way he might have gone?"

"Not really," replied the goat, "but since you are asking, why don't we take the left fork up here. If we go straight ahead we will soon reach those mountains and I'm thinking the Prankster would go where he thought there might be people on which to pull his nasty pranks!"

"Sounds okay to me," Barney replied. "What about it, fellows?" he asked, turning to the monkeys.

They both shrugged and gave their monkey grins. They walked the short distance to the cross roads and turned left.

"Say," said Billy, "how will Callie know which way we've gone?"

Immediately the two monkeys began scampering around gathering up sticks and small stones and soon they had constructed a nice arrow by the side of the road pointing to the left.

"How did Farf and Nurf convince the Prankster to let them transport him?" asked Barney as they walked along. "I know they said they just tossed him in and did it. However, I don't think it would be that easy. I figure the more we know about that fellow before we find him, the easier it might be to get him to do what we want."

"Agreed," replied Art. "Farf and Nurf managed to get him into the taffy room and before he knew what they were up to, he was bound up in strings of taffy. Then they just hauled him to the machine and that was it."

"I would think we might find a pile of taffy lying around somewhere where he got out of the stuff," laughed Burt.

"Perhaps the wild critters came by and ate it," suggested Two-Bits.

They had covered a few miles when they saw several jack rabbits racing toward them, their ears laid back and their frightened eyes bulging.

"Run, run, run!" shouted the first rabbit as he raced by them.

"Turn around quick before it gets you!" exclaimed the second.

"It will eat you, the glowing thing will," shouted the third rabbit as he raced along in the wake of his friends. Several more rabbits went by at a fast rate of speed. Then they were over the hill and gone.

"I wonder what that was all about," said Barney.

"Don't know," replied Two-Bits. "I just know that rabbits get frightened easily over the least important things. I'd say it was nothing."

They had walked another two hundred paces or so when they heard a loud thrashing in the bushes near the road. They stopped and waited expecting something to appear. Nothing came out of the thick growth.

"Come on out, friend," called Two-Bits. "We can hear you in there."

"Gah-ghe-ga-ga," came the reply.

"You wait here and I'll check it out," said Two-Bits. "I haven't had the opportunity to butt anything yet and I'd like to try out these horns."

Barney laughed. "Go right ahead. We'll just wait right here."

Two-Bits trotted off the road and up the gentle slope where there was a good stand of trees and bushes. Without hesitation, he entered the vegetation.

A moment later, the goat's head poked out of the bushes and he called for his companions to join him.

"Well, my gosh," exclaimed Barney when they had reached the grove, "what have we got here?"

Tangled in the bushes and tree roots that were exposed above the ground lay a man made of metal. Ropes were wrapped tightly around his ankles and his thighs. His arms were bound to his waist and more rope was wound about his upper arms. One piece of rope had even been placed within his mouth and tied to the back of his head, but the strange thing about the binding was that it glowed and shimmered, like something unreal or supernatural.

Barney and Billy took hold of the man and pulled him into a sitting position. Then they tried to take the gag rope from his mouth.

"Barney," exclaimed Billy in exasperation, "I can't untie this! I'm usually pretty good at this sort of thing."

"Here, let me try my pocketknife," said the farmer as he drew the knife from his pocket. He opened the blade and attempted to cut the cord. The brightly shining cord would not cut and it could not be untied.

"Well," said Barney, "let's get this tin fellow down to the road where we can have more room to work. Then we'll see if we can't get him free of this rope."

Together they lifted the tin man who was rather heavy and carried him to the clear area beside the road. Then they tried again to untie the fellow and they tried again with the pocketknife. Neither worked.

All the bound man could say was "gah-ghe-ga-ga", which was no help at all.

Bouncer tried to chew through the binding but soon gave up as he made no progress with the ropes.

"Let's build a fire and see if the stuff will burn," suggested Billy. They soon learned that the cord would not burn and again they were stumped.

"I believe," said Two-Bits, "that we are looking

at another one of the Prankster's tricks! That fellow is just plain nasty!"

The metal man was shaking his head vigorously in agreement.

"How did you get into those bushes up there?" Barney asked. "Is that where the Prankster left you?"

The man carefully shook his head negatively and then he slowly stretched out flat on the ground and began to roll. He could actually roll as fast as a man could walk. He rolled around in a circle and came back to his original spot and sat up.

"So you have been rolling around the country and finally got caught up there in the bushes, is that it?"

The man nodded.

"Are you the Tin Man?" Barney asked suddenly. "I remember Bertha reading about you when the kids were younger!"

The bound fellow shook his head.

"Are you made of tin?" the farmer asked.

The man nodded affirmatively.

"How long have you been rolling around like this?" asked Billy.

Slowly the tin fellow began winking one eye. Billy began counting.

"For over two weeks you've been bound like this!" exclaimed the farmer when the tin man stopped winking. "I take it you do not eat food or drink water?" he asked and the fellow shook his head.

It was about this time that Bouncer and the two monkeys went toward the nearby trees to play.

While the monkeys were actually men, they still had a little bit of monkey in them and at the moment they felt like playing.

Once they were within the trees, the monkeys quickly climbed into the branches and began swinging about the forest. Bouncer ran along below them barking and yipping. The little greyhound was having a great time with his new friends.

So it was, the more they played, the deeper they wandered into the forest which grew thicker and darker as they went inward.

In a short time they came to a stream of water. Bouncer did not need a drink since he was made of wire, but the two monkeys were thirsty and came down from the trees for a drink. Unmindful of where they were going or how long they had been gone, they crossed the brook and continued their frolic. Not far beyond the stream, Bouncer held his nose up to the breeze wafting gently behind them.

"Do you smell something?" he asked.

The two monkeys checked the breeze but neither had senses acute enough to pick up anything out of the ordinary.

"I think there is something behind us," said Bouncer. "I wonder how far we are from Barney and Billy?"

The two monkeys looked at each other with perplexed looks. Neither of them knew just where they had left their friends.

"Do you know how to get back?" asked Burt.

"It seems we should go that way," said Art, pointing to his right.

"I thought it was back that way, toward the

creek," said Bouncer.

There came a rustle in the bushes not far behind them. The monkeys' eyes widened perceptibly. Then came a low growl.

The two monkeys scampered up the nearest tree. Bouncer clawed at the trunk but greyhounds don't climb trees and he was stuck on the ground.

Emerging from the bushes a short distance away was a huge burley bear. The beast lumbered toward them, licking his chops as he approached.

Art and Burt, responding to their human instincts, suddenly rushed down the tree trunk, grasped Bouncer and hustled back to safety in the higher branches. The little dog gasped a sigh of relief and then clutched frantically to the swaying branches for he had never been in a tree in his short existence.

The big burley bear clawed his way a few feet off the ground and then slid back to the sod. He was far too big to climb the tree. He sat back on his rump and looked into the branches, his jowls drooling as he looked at what he hoped would be his dinner.

Art, Burt, and Bouncer waited for some time, hoping the big brute would go away. When it became apparent the fellow was prepared to wait them out, they decided to swing through the trees in an effort to lose him. The two monkeys took hold of the wire dog and they began traversing the treetops. They stayed as high as they could in the trees to stay out of sight of the burley bear trying to follow them on the ground.

"I haven't caught the bear's scent for quite some

time now," said Bouncer. "Perhaps we should go lower and see if we have lost him."

The monkeys did as their little friend suggested. Sure enough there was no bear in sight. Bouncer was anxious to get his feet back on solid ground.

"I think it's time we got back to Barney and Billy," said Bouncer, once they were out of the trees.

The monkeys agreed and they set off immediately, although they were not exactly sure which way they should be going.

They had not gone far when Bouncer's nose began to twitch again. "Do you catch anything on the breeze?" he asked.

Art and Burt tensed, ready to spring for the nearest tree. "Is it the burley bear again?" they whispered.

"No," replied Bouncer. "I don't know what it is."

There was a crackling twig behind them and they turned quickly. Standing in a long line were a dozen little purple tinted men. They were dressed in skins and carried primitive spears. The creatures had large ears and a mane of bristle like hair standing up on their heads and continuing down their backs.

Bouncer and his friends turned immediately in the opposite direction and found themselves facing another dozen of the little people. They were surrounded. Soon the monkeys had their hands bound and a rope was placed about Bouncer's neck.

They were led away into the forest.

CHAPTER FIFTEEN:
THE MAGIC BOOK IS MISSING!

Woot, the Wanderer, the Shaggy Man, and the Tin Woodman followed the winding trail in the Woot Wagon. They went up and down ridges and crossed streams which, now that they did not need them, seemed to be in abundance. They traveled through beautiful country and the scenes were often breath taking.

"It certainly makes one glad to be alive," observed the Shaggy Man.

"I am glad that I chose the life of a wanderer," replied Woot. "How can one compare the beauty and peacefulness that we have witnessed with anything else?"

"I enjoy the beauty and the serenity," offered the Tin Woodman, "but what I enjoy most is the company of good friends. And I certainly have that!"

They traveled steadily and by midafternoon, decided to stop the Woot Wagon and take a break to stretch their legs. Woot picked a beautiful glade near the trail and rolled his vehicle to a stop.

The boy and the Tin Woodman were discussing the beauty of several flowers that were growing nearby when the Shaggy Man decided to take another look at the thick book they had picked up in the cave. He checked the large pockets of his shaggy outfit but it was not there. He was not overly concerned and returned to the Woot Wagon, as they now consistently called the Spring-O-Wagon, to look through the storage areas under the seats. The book was missing.

"My friends," he called, "did either of you take the book we picked up from Tommy? It does not seem to be here."

"No," replied the Tin Woodman and Woot just shook his head. They both returned to the Woot Wagon and searched all three compartments but no book was to be found.

"Where could we have lost it?" asked Woot.

"Who had it last?" the Tin Man wanted to know.

After some discussion, it was decided that the last they knew of *The Prankster's Book of Phine Pranks* was just before Mara and Clara had visited their camp. No one had seen it since.

"I do recall the Guardian of the Waterfall saying that those two girls were in the habit of taking things that did not belong to them," said the Shaggy Man. "I wonder if they picked up the book?"

"Perhaps after we have located Captain Fyter,"

said the Tin Man, "and determined if he is in need of our help, we should return and see if the girls do, indeed, have our book."

"Perhaps the Captain would return with us to lend a bit of authority in retrieving the book," agreed the Shaggy Man.

They climbed aboard the Woot Wagon and continued on their journey. It was not long before they rolled around a curve in the trail and saw a large forested valley before them. Far away, beyond the valley, they could see a more level terrain and knew they were close to leaving the rugged country in which they were traveling.

Darkness came when they were about half way across the forested lowlands. Woot selected a clear spot beside the trail and brought his vehicle to a stop. The three companions went about setting up their camp site for the night and soon had a cheery little fire burning. Woot and the Shaggy Man had eaten and the Tin Woodman was in the process of oiling his joints when a weird cry floated through the dark trees.

"What was that?" exclaimed Woot. "I've never heard a cry like that?"

The Shaggy Man and the Tin Man listened intently but the cry did not come again. They both shook their heads, not knowing what it was.

"You know," said Woot, after another moment of listening, "I'm of a notion to walk out there a ways and see if there is anything unusual."

"Sounds like a recipe for excitement or a ticket to adventure," said the Shaggy Man, "and I've never been known to turn down either opportunity."

"In that case," said the Tin Woodman, putting his oil can inside his compartment designed especially for the container, "I shall accompany you with my axe. It may be that you will need our services."

Woot laughed at how ready his two friends were for excitement and adventure. He led the way and they walked quietly into the forest in the direction from which the strange noise had seemed to come.

They were perhaps two hundred paces into the dark shadowed forest and were nearing a pool that lay sparkling in the moonlight. They stopped at the edge of the clearing where the pool was located and stood silently for a long moment.

On the opposite side of the clear pool, a man sat on a large stone. His elbows were on his knees and he held his face in his hands. He was the picture of sadness.

"Well," said the Tin Woodman, "I say we should go around to the other side of the pool and cheer this fellow up!"

"He certainly looks sad," agreed Woot. "Perhaps we can learn what brings on his sadness and develop a remedy for it."

The Tin Woodman led his two friends around the pool and toward the sitting man. Presently the fellow raised his head and looked at them but gave very little indication that he saw them.

"Good evening, my friend," spoke the Tin Woodman. "We saw you sitting here and thought perhaps we could help you with your troubles, if you would care to share them with us."

The fellow gave a long sigh and turned his head

to look at the three strangers. Then he stood up. He was a tall man but he was also extremely lean and gaunt.

"Have you, by chance," he said, "seen two young girls? They have disappeared and we cannot find them! We have been searching for days and fear something dreadful has happened to them."

"Yes," said the Tin Woodman, "we have seen two young girls, but..."

"You have!" broke in the man, joy written all over his face. "Where? How long ago? Come quickly! We must tell Martha!" With that the overjoyed man grabbed the Tin Woodman by the arm and began pulling him along.

Woot and the Shaggy Man followed as the excited fellow led them toward a dark cabin far back in the shadows of the trees.

"Martha! Martha!" he yelled as they hurried along a cobblestone path leading toward the little cottage.

"I hope we have done the right thing," said the Shaggy Man. "That fellow is certainly building up high hopes."

A woman appeared in the doorway, her eyes red from weeping.

"They have seen the girls!" shouted the man.

"Where, George? Where?" cried the woman. "We must go to them immediately!"

"Where were they?" asked the man named George, turning to face the Tin Woodman. "Where did you see them?"

"We saw them night before last," the metal man replied, "on the trail just below the Falls of

Forbidden Water."

"Oh dear," the woman gasped. "Had they taken a drink of the water?"

"No, no," replied the Tin Woodman. "They did not drink of the water."

"The girl's names," said the Shaggy Man, "were Mara and Clara and they said they were in a hurry to get home when we talked with them."

The expression on the faces of the man and woman changed immediately. The sadness had returned.

"They are not our children," the man said. "Our little girls are much younger and they are named Trixie and Moxie."

"Oh, then perhaps the..." began the Tin Woodman, but stopped when he felt the Shaggy Man's hand on his shoulder.

"Let's not bother them," said the old man, "with your story just yet. Let us hear their story."

"Oh, yes," Nick Chopper replied. "I should remember my manners."

"When did your children disappear?" asked Woot.

"They have been gone many days now," the woman said. "It seems like a life time since they disappeared."

"Yes," the man agreed. "It was right after we were visited by that tall man in the heavy dark coat. He was very strange but I guess he was all right."

"I believe," said the Shaggy Man, choosing his words carefully, "this is a problem to be taken up with Princess Ozma. I live in the Emerald City and I shall be returning there before long. At that time I will have a conference with the Princess and I shall certainly bring up the plight of Trixie and Moxie. If anything can be done, Princess Ozma will do it."

"I believe you should have hope," added Woot. "Just believe that your little girls will be returned. They were twins, were they not?"

"Why, yes, how did you know?" questioned Martha.

At a hard look from the Shaggy Man, Woot just shrugged his shoulders. The old fellow was trying hard to alleviate the suffering of the mother and father without telling them about the condition of their children or bringing up the Prankster.

"Perhaps you would care for a cup of tea," Martha suggested. She turned and led the visitors into the little house.

"Have you made the acquaintance of one Captain Fyter?" asked the Shaggy Man a short time later as they enjoyed tea with their new friends.

"Why, yes," replied George. "We met the fellow once. I believe he was made out of tin, much as are you," he said, referring to the Tin Woodman.

"Ah, yes," replied Nick Chopper. "We are about as close to being brothers as one can get."

"We are searching for the Captain," said the Shaggy Man. "I take it you have not seen him recently?"

"It has been a long while since we have seen Captain Fyter," replied Martha. "Our cabin is not on the traveled road and we do not get many visitors."

"We heard a strange cry a short while ago," said Woot. "We were wandering this way in hopes of discovering its source."

"Oh," said George, "that was Martha. Sometimes when her sadness and anxiety gets too much to bear, she just cries out." There was silence for a moment.

"I am sorry," said Woot. "I did not mean to be rude."

"I think it best that we be getting back to our camp now," said the Shaggy Man. "In our search for Captain Fyter, if we should find your children, we will load them up and bring them back to you immediately."

"Load them up? What do you mean?" asked George.

"Our means of travel," explained the Shaggy Man, "is by the Woot Wagon. It is a vehicle that carries us along our way. We cover ground much faster than by walking."

George and Martha nodded and waved as the three adventurers walked away to return to their camp by the trail.

CHAPTER SIXTEEN:
CALLIE AND THE MAGIC BOOK

Callie Conniption arrived at the Candy Caverns on horseback with her foreman, Rusty. They reined their mounts to a stop and stepped down from the saddles to speak with the attendant at the gate.

"Good Morning, Miss Callie," the fellow called. "It's nice to have you visit us again. Farf and Nurf will be pleased."

"I need to see them right away," replied the cowgirl. "Is it all right to just go right on in?"

"Sure, it is," the fellow at the gate grinned.

"Rusty, you stay here with the horses. I'll come back and let you know if you're to go on back to the O-Bar-Z or if I'll be going with you."

"Oh, no you don't, Miss Boss Lady!" exclaimed Rusty. "I have a sweet tooth, too, you know!"

Callie laughed out loud. "I forgot," she said,

with a big smile. "Come on in. I'm sure there are plenty of cinnamon drops and I'll bet the attendant will be glad to watch our horses while they graze."

"I'd be delighted," the door man replied.

Callie and Rusty moved quickly through the Candy Caverns and into the kitchens. They helped themselves to their favorite pieces as they moved along and in moments were standing before the laboratory doors of Farf and Nurf. The two brothers appeared immediately upon Callie's knock, and were genuinely glad to see the pair from the O-Bar-Z.

"Callie!" exclaimed Farf. "We've been expecting you but thought it would be sometime tomorrow! Glad you're here."

"I expect you'll want to transport immediately," said Nurf and when Callie nodded her head, the man reached over and flipped the switch to start warming up the machine.

It seemed to Callie and Rusty that they had been visiting with their old friends for just a few moments when the Illuminator Transporter was ready.

"Callie," said Farf, "I did not have a belt small enough to give to Art and Burt so I trust that you will find them and when that Kansas farmer makes the Prankster change everybody back to their proper form, you'll bring my two enchanted candy makers back with you."

"Of course," replied Callie. "I've got my own book of magic right here," and she patted her pocket, "that we must get the Prankster to straighten out!"

Farf picked up a bright red belt that was trimmed with bronze colored wiring and was set with several golden studs. There was a silver button placed adjacent to the buckle that the twin pointed out as being the return button.

"Just push the button," he instructed, "and it will return you to this laboratory!"

"Just in case you get hungry," said Nurf, "I have put together a sack of your favorite candy, chocolate covered walnuts! Enjoy it as you follow the trail of the farmer!"

"Thanks," the girl said, taking the sack and fastening it to the side of her new belt. Then she turned to her riding companion.

"Rusty," said Callie, reaching out to shake her foreman's hand, "take care of things until I get back. Why don't you ask if you can just stable my horse here and then I'll have transportation back to the ranch when I return?"

"No problem there," responded Nurf. "We'll take care of it."

"Are you ready?" asked Farf.

"Ready as I reckon I'll ever be," the girl commented as she stepped toward the Illuminator Transporter.

"I'm going," said Rusty quickly. "I can't stand to watch this," and with that the foreman hurried from the room.

The cowgirl came to her senses as she was slowly descending toward the green turf below her. On the distant horizon she could see the purple of mountains and thought to herself that she was indeed in Gillikin Country. Where the Munchkin

Country has a blue tinge to many of the plants, flowers and other denizens, the Gillikin Country would have a slight purple tinge to various species of life.

When Callie had her feet solidly on the ground, she took a deep breath and started toward what appeared to be a road a short distance away. Briefly she wished she had been able to bring her horse but that was impossible because there wasn't any way to get it into the Illuminator Transporter. She lengthened her stride, determined to catch up with Barney and company.

In a short time she came to the crossroads and, seeing the arrow sign on the ground, smiled as she turned to the left, also. However, the cowgirl had not traveled far when she heard singing, accompanied by the notes of a flute, coming from a grove of trees on a hillside. Pausing only a moment, she determined to check out the source of the music and then get back on the trail of her friends.

Callie approached the trees with caution. The musical notes and the singing continued to float softly on the breeze but she did not seem to be any closer to the source. She entered the trees, following the sound of the music.

The cowgirl passed through the stand of trees and the sound seemed to be coming from another grove of big trees not far distant. She stopped with half a mind to return to the trail but decided she might learn something from whoever was making the music. She continued onward.

She passed through a second grove and seemed to be no nearer to the music makers than before.

Now she was determined to see this thing through. With a hard look of determination on her face, she continued striding along following the sound of the music.

It was just past noon when she came to a babbling brook and on the bank, sat two young girls. One was playing the flute and the other was singing as she absentmindedly paged through a book.

"Howdy, girls," called Callie as she walked into the clearing. Immediately the two youngsters leaped to their feet. The book dropped unnoticed to the grassy turf.

They backed away carefully for a moment, uncertainty written on their faces. Then their confidence seemed to return and they smiled at the cowgirl.

"What is your name?" one of the girls asked.

"I'm Callie," replied the tall redhead. She removed her wide brimmed Stetson and stepped forward, her hand outstretched.

"I'm Mara," said the girl, who appeared to be the oldest, as she moved to greet the friendly stranger.

"I am Clara," said her sister, standing just behind Mara's shoulder.

"Perhaps you can help me out," said Callie with a big smile on her face. "I am trying to find a group made up of a man, a boy, a goat, and two monkeys. I wonder if you may have seen them?"

"I don't think so," replied Mara, laughing. "We did see an old man, a young man, and a tin man a few days ago. However, we have seen no one since.

We are on our way south to visit our aunt and stopped here to rest for a while."

"Oh," said Callie, "I see you were also reading." She moved over and picked up the book from the ground. Immediately she saw that it looked like a book of magic in that is was well bound and had a clasp for locking the covers.

"No, no," said Mara. "We just found the book. We can't read. That's a waste of time, you know."

"Oh," said Callie as she saw the title, *The Prankster's Book of Phine Pranks*. "Perhaps you would let me have the book since I can read."

The two girls looked at each other, then Mara shook her head. "I think we will keep it. After all, we did find it."

"Tell you what," said Callie, realizing that she must get possession of the book, even if she had to take it by force. "I have a bag of very good chocolate candy on my belt. I will give you one piece each for the book you cannot read."

The girls were tempted and they put their heads together and whispered for a moment. Then Mara turned to Callie.

"We want three pieces each and then you are to..." began Mara.

"That's a hard bargain," broke in Callie, putting a stop to the demands.

"Well, that's what we have to have," said Mara, reaching out to take the book from the cowgirl. Callie casually backed away and ignored the outstretched hand.

"Tell you what," said Callie. "I'll give you one piece. I'll break it in half so that you can each eat part of it. After you eaten it, you can tell me if you still want to trade."

So saying, the young woman opened her sack and removed a piece of the candy which she broke in two and handed to the girls. They popped the morsels into their mouths quite greedily.

"All right," said Callie after the girls had finished their samples. "What do you think? Do you want to trade?"

Both girls nodded their heads vigorously. Callie handed each of them three pieces of the chocolate covered walnuts.

"I must be going now," she said, wanting to get away from the girls as soon as possible. There was something she did not like about the pair.

"Goodbye," she called to the two girls who were stuffing their faces with the candy she had given them. They did not seem to know that Callie had left.

The cowgirl moved steadily and with a feeling of urgency in retracing her route back to the road. She had gone some distance when she chanced to look back and caught a glimpse of the girls following her.

"They are either after the book or the candy," she murmured. "We'll see about this," she said, beginning to move in a wide loop. Presently she came to the brook as it tumbled along. She sat down by the edge and removed her boots and then stepped into the water. She gave the appearance with her tracks as going upstream. When the water was ankle deep and flowing quite strongly, she turned and went downstream.

Walking on the gravel and rocks of the river bed was tough on the cowgirl's feet. After a quarter of a mile, Callie left the stream and moved straight away from it at right angles, being careful to cover her tracks as well as she could.

She never saw the sisters again.

Estimating as to where she would come again to the road being taken by her friends, she moved along rapidly. By late afternoon she was traveling through some rugged hill country and had decided the trail had taken a turn before reaching the hills.

Callie was tired, as she had pushed herself to put as much distance between her and the sisters as possible. When she saw a small cave on the slope of a rocky hill, she decided to check it out with the possibility of spending the night in it. The small den seemed to be just right and did not appear to be occupied by any of the critters of the wild. She immediately started a small fire and leaned back to relax. In short order, she was sound asleep.

Callie slept that evening and through the night. She awakened the following morning as the sun was rising. Her first thought was that she had wasted a day. The next thought was that she was cold. She gathered some fuel and got her fire going again. Then as she warmed up, she opened up the book that had been the source of the lost day. Her eyes opened wide as she began reading. She flipped to the back pages of the journal and looked at the handwritten list that filled those pages. The fire died down and she added more twigs without leaving the book.

Hours passed and during that time she pulled

out her own book of magic and made changes where the Prankster had pulled his troublesome jokes. From the list in the back of the book, she looked up the remedy for each and every prank the Prankster had pulled. At long last, she stood up and stretched, a satisfied smile on her pretty face.

"I think I am ready!" Callie said exuberantly. She took a piece of candy from her pouch and popped it in her mouth. Then the girl set out in the direction she thought would intersect the path Barney and his friends were following.

*****

The Purple Scamps, as they were called, came to a patch of plum bushes and stopped to pick the ripe purple fruit. It was sweet and juicy and they soon tied Bouncer to a nearby tree. Then they added the two monkeys on tether ropes of their own and the entire band became very busy picking and eating the fruit.

In short order, Bouncer had chewed through the bindings on Art's hands and he in turn, untied the rest of the knots and the three animals slipped away unnoticed by the Purple Scamps.

A greyhound and two monkeys can be extremely fast when the necessity arises and it was just moments before Bouncer, Burt, and Art were far away from the plum pickers. Swinging in a wide loop the three companions moved in what they hoped was the right direction for them to find Barney Fields.

It was not long before they caught sight of a tall lean figure striding along. Quickly they took cover in the brush and watched.

"That's Callie!" exclaimed Art as he bounced to his feet and rushed out to meet the young lady.

When Callie saw the first monkey bounding toward her followed by yet another monkey and that one trailed by a little dog, her first thought was to run.

Then she remembered that two candy makers had been turned into monkeys and the little dog certainly looked like Barney's dog, Bouncer. At about the same time she understood the monkeys calling her by name and turned toward them.

"Callie! Callie! Are we glad to see you," exclaimed Art as he followed his monkey's intuition and leaped into the young lady's arms. He was followed by Burt while Bouncer remained on the ground, bouncing.

"Boy, do I have good news for you!" Callie cried breathlessly. "Are you ready to be turned back into your normal forms?"

"Yes! Yes!" the two monkeys replied ecstatically.

"All right," said Callie. "Here is what you do. First, look me in the eyes and do not look away!" It took only a few minutes before the cowgirl had both of the candy makers changed back to their own forms.

"Wow, this feels good!" said Art.

"Callie," beamed Burt, "we are in your debt for life!"

Callie laughed happily with the two men and while Bouncer was pleased for them he also missed his monkey friends.

"Which way do we go to find Barney and Two-

Bits?" Callie asked.

Art and Burt looked at each other and then back to Callie. "To be honest, we were lost," said Art.

"However, we thought it was that way," added Burt, pointing.

"My thoughts, too," replied the cowgirl. "Let's go."

CHAPTER SEVENTEEN: THE GOLDEN BOX

It took only an hour for Callie, the candy makers and Bouncer to discover the road they were sure was the one Barney and Two-Bits were traveling.

"Now," said Art, "if we just knew which way to go. I don't remember this scenery so they are probably that way," and he pointed to the left.

"However," said Burt, "if they continued down the road, thinking we'd catch up when we returned, they could be quite a ways in that direction," and he pointed to the right.

"Gosh, if we could just yell out and get an answer how simple it would be," said Callie.

"Why not?" said Art and he immediately cupped his hands to his mouth and yelled in a very loud voice. "Barney! Barney Fields!"

Dismay covered the faces of the three people

when they heard Barney's answer in reply, just beyond the rise to their left. Quickly they hurried in that direction.

When they topped the rise they found Barney and Two-Bits along with the bound Captain Fyter stretched out on the ground.

"Callie!" exclaimed Barney, waving to the cowgirl as they approached. "Sure glad to see you! Who are these two strangers you have with you?"

The two men were grinning from ear to ear. "I'm Art," the closer one said.

"I'm Burt," added the second one. "Callie found a way to lift the Prankster's spells! Are you ready, Two-Bits?"

"Oh, boy, am I ever!" the goat exclaimed. "You can do it this time, huh, Callie?"

"I certainly think so," she replied. "Come over here and look me right in the eyes, very steadily. Don't look away for anything!"

It took Callie just a few moments and the goat was a reindeer.

"You have my eternal gratitude," said the deep throaty voice of Two-Bits' reindeer voice. "Finally," he added, "my head feels right! I really missed my rack of antlers!"

"I'm glad it worked right this time," the girl said. "I really felt bad about the first time we tried."

"Callie," said Barney, "is there anything you can do for our metal friend here?" The farmer indicated the form of the man on the ground bound with the magic rope.

Callie looked at the fellow and then pulled the book from her pocket. She thumbed to the pages in the back.

"I believe you are Captain Fyter, are you not?" she asked and the man nodded his head vigorously.

The cowgirl looked in the book some more and then shook her head slowly. "According to this manual, I need another source of magic to break the spell of the rope. I am one source but we'll need someone else who can work some magic. I think we may have to wait until we can get you to the Emerald City," explained the redheaded girl.

They heard a shout and looked up to see a strange looking contraption rolling across the grass toward them. As it drew closer they could see a young man, who appeared to be in control of the machine, sitting on a stool near the front with his hands on a pair of handle bars not unlike a bicycle. On the second bench sat a tin man similar to the one lying securely bound on the ground. The third bench held an old man with long hair and beard flying in the breeze caused by the speed of the vehicle.

As the Woot Wagon rolled to a stop and its occupants stepped down, they saw the bound figure on the ground.

"Captain Fyter!" exclaimed the Tin Woodman. "Why is he being held a prisoner?" he asked of the group standing beside his friend.

"We've done all we can," answered Barney. "We can't remove the bindings!"

"Let me try," said Nick Chopper, moving quickly to the side of his friend. A few moments later the Tin Woodman was as stymied as the rest of the group.

"We need two sources of magic," explained the cowgirl. "I believe we can free him just as soon as we find a second person of magic."

"Let me introduce myself," said the shabbily dressed old man from the cart. "I am the Shaggy Man from the Emerald City where I am sometimes known as the Royal Traveler of Oz, among other things," he chuckled. "I am traveling with my friends, His Royal Highness, the Emperor of the Winkie Country," and he motioned toward the Tin Woodman, who took a deep bow. "And the third member of our party is Woot, the Wanderer and the owner of this magnificent piece of equipment that we have dubbed the Woot Wagon." Woot was smiling broadly.

"I am Art," said one of the two men standing next to the newcomers, "and this is my friend and fellow candy maker, Burt. We are from the Candy Caverns quite some distance from here in the Munchkin Country. We had been transformed into a pair of monkeys and joined our present group in search of a remedy. Fortunately, Miss Callie has come up with the solution to the Prankster's tricks and we are now back to our original forms."

"I am Callie," said the cowgirl. "I'm the boss of the O-Bar-Z Ranch and years ago I did practice a little magic. The Prankster visited our ranch and managed to foul up my book of magic so I came looking for him!" They all nodded in understanding.

The group then turned to Barney, who cleared his throat.

"Well," said the farmer, "I'm retired. I went to an auction where I ran into Billy and Two-Bits and shortly after we were caught in a rainstorm and brought here to Oz by way of a flying horse tank. Two-Bits had suffered from one of the Prankster's pranks and we, that is Billy and I, decided to see what we could do to help our friend. We had already been through quite a bit together."

Billy was standing beside the farmer who had placed his arm across the boy's shoulder.

"Don't forget about me," came a voice from the ground. Barney looked down to see his little wire greyhound sitting at his feet.

"Oh, yes," replied the farmer. "We stopped at Pamela's Pies for a bite to eat and I got to messing around with some baling wire Billy had found in a ditch and came up with Bouncer here." He reached down and gently picked up the dog.

"Barney!" exclaimed Callie. "You performed magic! You are our second source! We should be able to free Captain Fyter!"

"That's right," exclaimed Billy. "Have you still got that little golden box?" he asked.

"Yeah, I think so," murmured Barney as he fumbled at the pocket of his bib overalls. "Here it is," he said, lifting the little box up for all to see.

"Show them the little book!" said Billy in his excitement.

Carefully, holding the golden box just right, Barney popped the lid open and lifted out the little book titled *The Laughing Dragon of Oz*. Callie reached out for the small book and the farmer handed it to her. She looked at it carefully.

"You say there is magic to this book?" she asked.

"Yep," replied Billy. "That's how we got Bouncer here. He has been pretty valuable to us since he came to life."

"I'll say," said Burt and Art nodded in agreement. They were thinking of the little dog chewing their binding loose earlier when they had been held by the Purple Scamps.

"Let's give it a try," said Callie, handing the book back to Barney.

"What do I do?" asked Barney. "You're the expert here."

"The way I understand it, you just have to be there," said Callie. "Whatever it takes to break the spell will be drawn from your magic source. If the book is magic, I think we should just lay it on Captain Fyter as I try to nullify the magic of the ropes binding him."

Barney Fields walked over to the bound soldier and, sitting down beside him, placed the book on his chest.

"Just in case I have to be in close proximity," he said. "Like at Pamela's counter."

"Look at me," said Callie to the tin soldier. "Don't take your eyes from mine all through the process. The cowgirl repeated a few phrases that were unintelligible, all the while looking straight into the eyes of Captain Fyter.

Presently, the bound man flexed his arm and the ropes popped apart. He reached up and pulled the gag rope from his mouth. Then he sat up and reached down to his bound legs. Taking hold of the rope with his hands, he lifted and the strands snapped apart. Each time he removed a rope, he placed it in a pile beside him. All the while he maintained his eye contact with Callie.

"We are finished now," said Callie when the ropes were all removed. "You are a free man, Captain Fyter!"

"I thank you very much," were the first words from the tin soldier's mouth. "Should you ever need my services, you need only ask!"

Barney had caught his little book as it began to tumble when the tin man sat up. Now he replaced it in the golden box and carefully tucked it inside the bib pocket of his overalls.

CHAPTER EIGHTEEN: PIECES OF THE PUZZLE

The group gathered around Captain Fyter clapping him on the back and shaking his hand. The magic inflicted on him had been stronger than the spells cast on the other victims of the Prankster.

"I'm hungry," Billy finally said, as the excitement began to wear down.

"I am, too," said Woot. "Let's take the Woot Wagon and scout around the area a bit. Surely there is something edible growing close by!"

Billy and Woot got on the vehicle and, with a wave to their friends, began a search of the area.

"I'm anxious to get back to the Candy Caverns," said Burt, sometime later as he looked in Callie's direction.

"Me, too," chimed in Art.

Callie nodded that she understood and soon

came to stand by the two candy makers. She unfastened the bright red belt given her by Farf and handed it to the two men.

"I'm sure you know how to work it," she said and they nodded.

"We have made numerous trips using a return belt," said Art, "but you're going back with us, aren't you?"

"No," said Callie, slowly shaking her head. "In the back of the Prankster's book was a list of all the people and places on which he has cast some type of magic spell. I have helped those around me. But I believe Princess Ozma should have this book with the listing of the Prankster's malicious mischief. Since I can undo some of it, I should go to her with the book and see if I can be of help."

Both Art and Burt nodded. They certainly understood how others would feel while under the Prankster's spells.

Two-Bits, the reindeer, ambled over to the two candy makers, his huge rack of antlers swaying from side to side as he walked.

"Did I hear you mention returning to the Candy Caverns?" he asked. "Do you suppose I could transport with you and maybe Farf and Nurf could send me right back to the land of Kris Kringle?"

"I don't see why not," Art replied.

"How quickly do you plan to leave?" asked Two-Bits.

"We're ready now," said Burt, holding up the red belt.

"Fine," the reindeer replied, "however, if you don't mind, I'd like to say goodbye to Billy before I leave."

"We'll wait," the two men nodded.

It was not long before Billy and Woot returned with a considerable amount of nuts, berries and plums they had gathered. There was quite enough for the entire group.

"Billy," said the reindeer, "I am about to transport with Art and Burt. From the Candy Caverns, I will be sent directly to Santa Land. I will be so glad to be home!"

"Gosh, Two-Bits," said Billy, "we're gonna miss you! Will you ever come back?"

"I don't know," replied the reindeer. "This experience was enough to make one think twice about leaving home! However, I have a deep feeling you and I will see each other again!"

Billy rubbed his friend's forehead and antlers and swallowed a lump in his throat. Then Burt and Art came forward.

"Ready, Two-Bits?" one of them asked.

Two-Bits bobbed his head. The two candy makers moved in close, one on each side of the reindeer's rack of antlers. The two men took hold of the animal and then Burt pressed the button on the belt he had strapped about his waist. Slowly a strange light appeared about the three-forms. Then they seemed to become transparent and were floating a short distance off the ground. Finally there was a loud pop. Burt, Art and Two-Bits were gone.

The rest of the afternoon was spent in preparing and eating the food gathered by Woot and Billy. Callie said she knew how to use the nuts in such a manner as to make a stew that tasted like beef stew.

Nick Chopper and Captain Fyter had many adventures to relate since they had last met. The Shaggy Man and Woot were very interested in Barney and Billy and how they happened to be in Oz.

Callie turned her attention to the leather bound book that had been in the possession of the Prankster. Finding a spot in the shade of a tree, she sat down and began looking through the pages. Presently a shadow fell across the pages and she looked up to see the Shaggy Man peering intently at the book.

"Hi," she said and rose to her feet.

"I was wondering," the old man replied, "if you would care to tell me where you got that book. It looks strangely familiar to one I once had." He chuckled, then added, "However briefly."

"Sure," replied Callie and she proceeded to tell the Shaggy Man how she came into possession of *The Prankster's Book of Phine Pranks*. The old man nodded for a moment, then looked straight at Callie.

"Do you have any idea what this Prankster fellow might look like?" he asked.

"Oh, yes," Callie replied. "He stayed on the O-Bar-Z for a short while so I got to know him very well! He was tall and lean with a dark complexion. Big flowing mustache and long hair on the sides, but the hair on top of his head was cropped short, and he was always wearing a long black coat with pockets that contained all sorts of things. Oh, yes, the coat was trimmed in gold!"

"Did the fellow have an actual name of any

sorts?" the Shaggy Man asked.

"I believe he did," said the girl, her forehead furrowed in thought. "Yes, at times he would refer to himself as Tommy."

"It is fitting together," said the Shaggy Man. "Now I have a story for you."

"Shaggy Man," called Nick Chopper. "Captain Fyter and I have been discussing the problem of the Prankster. The man must be stopped from plying his tricks around the countryside where ever he pleases."

"Yes," added Captain Fyter as he drew his sword and checked its sharpness. "I shall start immediately in an effort to determine the Prankster's location."

"Just a moment," broke in the Shaggy Man. "Let me share with you the information Miss Callie and I have just put together. It makes for a rather interesting story." He looked around the clearing and motioned for the others to join them. They moved closer to the fire that Barney had just started and seated themselves on stones that Woot and Billy had rolled into place. The sun was sinking as the Shaggy Man began telling the story of what had happened to the Prankster.

"So it seems," the Shaggy Man concluded sometime later, "the fellow known as the Prankster got what he deserved. The Guardian of the Forbidden Waters says the man will be a much better and totally different person when he has gone through rehabilitation."

The small group sat quietly for some time, each immersed in their own thoughts.

"This has all really been exciting," Billy finally said. "It was never this much fun traveling around with those two hoboes who ditched me! What do we do next?"

"I think," said the Shaggy Man, "it would be proper for George and Martha to be told now what has happened to their two little girls and that they will soon be reunited with their parents and in the proper form."

"I shall bear that duty," said Captain Fyter. "This country is my responsibility and I would be happy to let them know all is going to turn out all right!"

With that the Captain stood and thanked Callie and Barney once again for breaking the spell of the magic ropes. Then he marched away into the darkness that had fallen since as a metal man he had no need for sleep.

"How did those cubs, or little girls, get so far away from their home?" asked Woot.

"Part of the spell the Prankster used on them was to zap them a thousand miles from their home! He was just plain mean!" replied Callie.

"Well," said the Shaggy Man, as he stretched, "I suggest we get a good night's sleep so that we can be on our way early tomorrow morning."

CHAPTER NINETEEN:
THE EMERALD CITY

Although they traveled through beautiful country and saw many unusual sights, the trip from the far reaches of the Gillikin Country was uneventful. It did, however, give Barney, Billy, and Callie ample time to become well acquainted with their new friends.

It was near midday on the third day of travel when the Woot Wagon rolled to the top of a hill and brought its riders into sight of the magnificent spires reaching skyward from the Emerald City.

Barney Fields and Billy were amazed at the grandeur of the great city long before they reached the gate and were greeted by Omby Amby, the Captain General of the Royal Army of Oz who stood by the Emerald Gates of the Royal City.

"Boy, oh, boy, look at that fellow," Billy

whispered to Barney. The Captain General was seven feet tall and sported a lush green beard that reached all the way to his feet.

"That is Omby Amby," said the Shaggy Man who had heard Billy's whisper. "He is the guard at the gate and we will stop and speak to him as he is a good friend."

Sure enough, Woot brought the Woot Wagon to a stop and they were greeted pleasantly by the guard. He asked how their trip had gone and then said the Princess Ozma was expecting them. With a long thin arm, he waved them onward.

"How did the Princess know we were coming?" Billy asked.

"She has a Magic Picture that can show her anyone at any time in the entire Land of Oz She very likely checked on the whereabouts of either the Tin Woodman or myself," said the Shaggy Man. "Then she would have seen all of us riding on the Woot Wagon on our way to the Emerald City."

Woot's amazing Woot Wagon had carried all six of its passengers with no trouble. It rolled just as fast as it did when there were only three riders on it.

Callie Conniption was almost as awed by the capital city of Oz as were Barney Fields and his young friend, Billy. The cowgirl had never been to the Emerald City.

Woot rolled his vehicle with care among the streets as they worked their way through the great numbers of people and other individuals who lived, worked and played in the fabled city of Oz. Eventually he brought the Woot Wagon to a stop before the great palace where the fairy princess

Ozma held court.

The party was met at the door by a pair of retainers and ushered immediately to the great throne room of the palace. Word was sent to the Hungry Tiger that the Shaggy Man and Nick Chopper had arrived.

"Would you look at that!" exclaimed Billy, as they stood just outside the throne room and looked through huge arched doorway. Princess Ozma was seated on her throne and on the dais beside her lay the Cowardly Lion who was huge and imposing. Scattered about the room were several scribes who were taking down names of various individuals along with their problems to be brought before the fairy princess.

A messenger approached the throne and whispered to Ozma, who immediately looked toward the doorway. Seeing the Shaggy Man and Nick Chopper, she smiled brightly and waved.

The Princess of the Emerald City stood up and the chattering, buzzing room became quiet.

"A matter of utmost urgency has just arrived," stated the young ruler. "I shall leave the courts for a short while. Please carry on until I return." With that she stepped down from the dais and moved toward a side door.

The Shaggy Man and Nick Chopper immediately led their party away from the doorway of the throne room and followed a circular hall that eventually came to the private quarters of Princess Ozma.

The young ruler was waiting for them just inside the entrance. By her side stood the great form of the

Hungry Tiger. At his feet sat the bear cub and the leopard cub, Trixie and Moxie.

"I am very glad to see you, Shaggy Man and Nick Chopper," the young princess said with sincerity, "and you too, Woot. It has been some time since you have visited the Royal Palace."

"Yes it has," agreed Woot. "My wanderings have taken me far and I have seen many strange places."

"Princess Ozma," said the Shaggy Man with dignity. "We have here Miss Callie Conniption of the O-Bar-Z Ranch and her two friends Barney Fields and Billy. They are from Kansas!"

"Oh, yes," smiled the princess, "I know some nice people from Kansas."

The three visitors were somewhat tongue tied and the young ruler turned immediately to the task at hand, that of returning the two cubs to their original forms.

"I would suggest," said the Shaggy Man, "that we just let Callie do her magic thing as she knows exactly what to do."

"Would you?" asked the fairy princess, turning to the cowgirl.

"I'd be happy to," replied Callie, a flush of excitement on her face.

In less time than it takes to tell about it, Callie Conniption knelt on the floor by the two cubs and instructed them to look deep into her eyes and not look away until she was through with the chant. They did as they were instructed and the red haired girl began uttering the meaningless magic words. That is, they were meaningless to everyone except

Princess Ozma, who listened with understanding and admiration.

Suddenly two young girls, about six years of age, stood by the Hungry Tiger. They looked at Ozma and tears began running down their little faces.

"There, there," said the fairy princess, as she patted them on their heads. "Let us check the magic picture to make sure it is safe and we will send you to your parents immediately."

Princess Ozma pulled the cords to the curtains that covered the magic picture on the wall. The beautiful pastoral scene was displayed for the waiting group and the young ruler asked immediately to see the parents of Trixie and Moxie. The picture began to swirl as the colors seemed to run all over the area within the frame. As they settled down they gave a view of a man and woman talking to Captain Fyter in the front yard of a small cabin surrounded by tall stately pine trees.

"Wonderful," said the princess as she slipped on her Magic Belt. She stepped over to the twins and laid her hands on their heads. "Goodbye, my little friends," she said and suddenly they were gone.

Immediately the group turned to the picture on the wall and there were the twins running to their mother and father with outstretched arms. In the background stood Captain Fyter, a smile on his metal face. Then the picture faded.

"Now we have another matter of pressing importance," said the Shaggy Man. "Callie has come into the possession of the Prankster's book. In the back are listed all the individuals and places that he has cast under some spell."

Princess Ozma nodded and the cowgirl pulled the book out and handed it to the young ruler, a smile on her face. She would be glad to put the magic business behind her.

Princess Ozma flipped through the book for a moment and then looked at Callie. "Would you being willing to stay around for a while and help me straighten out as much of this as we can?" she asked.

"Well, of course..." began the red haired girl, not knowing exactly what to say but flattered that someone of Ozma's stature would ask for her assistance.

"We will do what we can to right these spells," said the princess, "then we will call in Glinda, the Good Witch of the South, to finish those you and I are unable to resolve."

"Pardon me," said the Tin Woodman, "I realize I have only been here for a few moments but I have been away from my castle for some time now and I feel that I should return as soon as possible. Woot has agreed to take me home on his Woot Wagon, but we shall both return as soon as it is convenient for a long visit!"

"You are my good and loyal friend, Tin Woodman," said the fairy princess. "I look forward to your return."

With a wave, Nick Chopper and Woot, the Wanderer, took their leave.

"Shaggy Man," said Ozma, "I believe you and my visitors have a story to tell and I am quite anxious to hear all about your journeys and adventures! Come," she added, leading the way into another luxurious room. "I shall have food prepared and you may tell me all that has happened."

CHAPTER TWENTY:
ALL'S WELL THAT ENDS WELL

The following morning Barney awoke and sat up in bed in the special room in the Emerald Palace that had been prepared for him and Billy. The old man stretched and looked over at the young lad sleeping so peacefully and wondered how long it had been since the boy had actually slept in a bed. Bouncer was curled up at the foot of the lad's bed just like a normal dog. Barney was sure the little wire fellow was becoming more and more like a real dog every day.

"Boy," he murmured softly, "I sure could do with a cup of coffee right about now."

"I could do with one of Pamela's Pies," came the boy's voice from across the room.

"I thought you were still asleep," said Barney, turning toward Billy.

"I haven't been asleep for quite a while," was the reply. "I've been lying here waiting for you to wake up."

"Oh," said the farmer. "Let's try out those showers and get into our clean clothes," he laughed and pointed to their newly washed, ironed and folded clothes stacked just inside the door.

A short while later, with Bouncer playing at their feet, they were wondering just where to go for breakfast when a light knock came at the door.

"Come in," called the farmer. "We're up."

The door opened a crack and the face of Jellia Jamb appeared.

"Good morning, Jellia," said Barney, as he and Billy had met the maid the previous evening.

"Good morning to you both," the girl replied. "There is breakfast on the lower level and when you have finished, Princess Ozma would like to meet with the two of you for a short while."

"Let's go," said Barney as Jellia disappeared. He reached over to the small table by the bed and picked up the golden box that contained the Big Little Book and slipped it into his bib pocket.

Having finished their breakfast, Barney, Billy, and Bouncer were ushered into a special room that Princess Ozma used to meet with small groups.

"Good morning," smiled the little fairy princess. "I hope you slept well."

"That we did," the farmer said and Billy nodded in agreement.

"I have asked you to meet with me this morning because I have some questions I need to ask of you. First, Barney, are you a magician?"

"No," said Barney, a perplexed look coming over his face. "I know nothing at all about magic."

Ozma smiled and nodded. She turned to the little wire greyhound playing around Billy's feet.

"Bouncer," she called gently. "Come here, boy," and she clapped her hands softly. Immediately the little dog leaped in the lap of the girl ruler.

"Yet," said the princess, "you made Bouncer out of baling wire and brought him to life. I think there may be some magic in you of which you are unaware."

"Never in all my life," said Barney, "has anything like that ever happened before. I still don't know what to think of it!"

"Would you tell me again just how it came about?" she asked.

Barney Fields, with the help of Billy, went through the events leading up to Bouncer coming to life.

"May I see your little book and the golden box in which you carry it?" she asked.

Barney nodded and pulled the box from his bib pocket. He started to turn the box just right so that he could open it when he saw the girl's hand reaching out. He handed the golden box to her and as soon as both of her hands touched the box the lid popped open immediately.

Princess Ozma gently removed the little book titled *The Laughing Dragon of Oz* and held it in her hands. A light came over the girl's face and she smiled and nodded to no one in particular. She turned the book over in her hands several times.

"Is this book important to you?" she asked of

Barney.

Barney hesitated for a moment wondering just how to answer and the princess spoke again.

"There is magic to the book," she said. "I can feel it and sometimes it is quite strong. It seems to fluctuate somewhat."

"Well," said Barney, "I bought it rather cheaply at an auction along with a couple of dozen other books. I was kind of thinking about using it to help Billy learn to read."

"I suspect the magic only works here in Oz," the princess said in a low voice as if she were talking to herself. She continued to hold the book, turning it slowly in her hands as she did so.

"So, Billy, you wish to learn to read?" the girl ruler asked.

Billy nodded silently, somewhat embarrassed that he could not read. Ozma sensed his feelings.

"Do not feel bad," she said. "Many of the citizens in my kingdom cannot read. It is, however, their choice. I will show you." With that she walked to the wall and gave a tug on an emerald cord decorated with golden thread.

A servant appeared and Ozma consulted with him quietly for a moment and he left. The princess turned back to Billy.

"Professor H. M. Wogglebug T. E. just happens to be in the Emerald City at this time and I have asked him to join us. The H. M. stands for Highly Magnified and the T. E. stands for Thoroughly Educated."

"Oh," replied the lad, "I was never very good in school!"

"That won't matter," replied Princess Ozma, "as Professor Wogglebug will tell you."

The fairy princess replaced the little book in the golden box and returned it to Barney. The farmer accepted the box and tucked it inside his bib pocket.

"You know," he said, "I'd just give you this book once Billy has learned to read, if you'd like to have it."

"That would be nice," the princess replied. "We have quite an extensive library, both here in the palace and at the Royal College of Oz. We have quite a collection of books pertaining to Oz and its various inhabitants. With your permission, I should like to add this one to it. That is," she said with a laugh, "after Billy has read it."

A servant signaled to Ozma from the door and she went to speak with him. When they finished, the man left and Ozma turned to her guests.

"Professor Wogglebug is in the Royal Gardens," she said happily, "and I have sent word that we shall join him shortly."

Led by Princess Ozma, Barney, Billy and Bouncer were soon among some of the loveliest plants and flowers they had ever seen. The blooms were large and very fragrant and of the most delicate of colors.

"Boy, would Bertha love this!" Barney exclaimed.

"Who, may I ask, is Bertha?" smiled the princess.

"Bertha is my wife and she just loves gardening and flowers," Barney answered. "She was at a club meeting when Billy and the mule and I were caught in that storm. I'm sure she's worried sick about where I am. I sure wish I was back there!"

"Pardon me," said Billy softly, "but where is Callie?"

"Oh, how thoughtless of me!" exclaimed the princess. "Callie is with the Wizard and they are busy straightening out the mess the Prankster made! Things are going quite well, I might add. That nasty fellow had been very busy but the two of them think they can have everything back to normal within the week."

"Yipes!" came a startled cry from Billy and Bouncer gave a quick bark.

Standing before them was a very grotesque monstrosity. It stood fully as tall as Barney and had long spindly legs and arms. A top hat sat on his head and his nose more nearly resembled a carrot than a nose.

"Meet Professor Wogglebug," said the princess with a silvery laugh.

"I understand you wish to read, young fellow," said the professor.

"Yes, sir," replied Billy. "Very much."

"Then you are in luck, my child," said the Wogglebug. He reached into his vest pocket and pulled out a pill. "Take this when you find some water and you shall find yourself capable of reading!" The giant bug smiled in his strange sort of way, tipped his tall hat, and moved on through the gardens.

"Barney Fields and Billy," said Princess Ozma, "you two have performed a great service for my kingdom and you are very good people. You are welcome to stay in our wonderful land or, as I heard Barney wish, I can return you to your home in Kansas! There could be other options, too. Now, it is time for me to go to the Royal Throne Room and take care of the day's activities."

Barney nodded. "Could we let you know our decision tomorrow?" he asked. "Billy and I have some things we'd like to do and see before deciding about returning to Kansas. This is such a beautiful city!"

"Certainly," smiled the princess, "you are welcome here as long as you wish to stay." Then she turned and moved swiftly toward the Emerald Palace.

"Barney," said Billy excitedly. "Let's find a water fountain so I can take this pill and then I want to read that Oz book to you!"

THE END

ABOUT THE AUTHOR

John was born and raised in the sand hills of south central Kansas. There were seven siblings and they grew up on a farm. When the weather cooperated, they raised cattle, horses, hogs, wheat and milo.

Both of John's parents liked to read, so they all grew up reading and listening to the many stories his mother would tell to keep them entertained as she did housework.

In the late forties and early fifties, they discovered radio programs, pulp magazines, big little books and comic books.

When he was about a fifth grader, John saw his first Tarzan movie and spent the next several days trying to get it all written down on paper. From that point on, he was usually involved in some type of story he was either telling or trying to write.

John has been married to his wife Meredith for over fifty years. They have two children. Mike lives in Colorado and Anne Marie lives in Arizona.

John's stories are usually westerns, space opera, sports, young adult or a combination of those. Yes, he does have one series that involves them all!

Made in the USA
Coppell, TX
17 February 2022